Veritas Series

CAT'S PAW
KILLING GAME
BROKEN DREAMS

BROKEN DREAMS

A Veritas Novel

Jana Oliver

 Nevermore Books

Published by
MageSpell, LLC
Coimbra, Portugal

This work is a novel of fiction. Names, characters, places, and incidents are the product of the author's imagination and are not to be construed as real. Any resemblance to actual persons, living or dead, events or locales, businesses or organizations is entirely coincidental.

BROKEN DREAMS
A Veritas Novella

ISBN: 978-1-941527-35-1
2nd Edition

Acknowledgments

An author can write a book, but it takes a village
to see it published.

Mollie Traver (www.MollieTraver.com)
served as content advisor and offered
both editorial and copy-editing expertise.

Melanie Fletcher (https://melaniefletcher.com/belaurient-arts)
who created the cover design.

~ Jana Oliver
August 2025

In an effort to make your reading experience
as enjoyable as possible, we have chosen not to
right margin justify the typeset text,
although this is industry standard.

Studies have shown that people with reading
difficulties, including those with dyslexia, find
it easier to follow free-flowing text, with better
reading comprehension as a result.

*"There are three classes of men;
lovers of wisdom,
lovers of honor,
and lovers of gain."*

~ Plato

Chapter One

Atlanta, Georgia
Monday, May 11th
9:45 p.m.

Samuel Marsh took a deep inhalation of the thick cocktail of car fumes and barbecue. The fumes reminded him of Chicago, his hometown, though the barbecue was uniquely Southern. Since he was in the heart of Atlanta, that was to be expected. It was approaching ten o'clock on a fine May evening, the temperature still in the upper seventies. A far cry from the fifties and sixties Chicago had been experiencing.

Rather than calling a cab Sam opted to walk the however many blocks to his hotel from the restaurant where he'd had a late supper. Walking always cleared his head, and he had a lot on his mind.

He was just beginning the second week of his vacation, and being a Civil War buff he'd spent it in the heart of the Old South. The previous week he'd drifted from Virginia to Georgia. It'd been a steady diet of museums and battlefields. The War Between the States, or the War of Northern Aggression as some Southerners still insisted upon calling it, had been a fascination of his since he was a kid. To spend fourteen days immersed in it felt like a gift he didn't deserve.

Also, it felt odd not being on assignment for Veritas. He'd worked as a freelance private investigator with them over the last year, and beginning on Monday he'd be full-time, a sea change from his time as a homicide detective. It'd been a good choice, considering he'd left the Chicago Police Department under a cloud, at least from his perspective.

Before each Veritas mission a comprehensive background dossier was compiled. Sam's job was to double check all the information contained in that report, be it online or in person. He had a head for that kind of mind-numbing detail, and found he really enjoyed the work. So far Veritas had been impressed with his efforts, and now he'd begun compiling the "backgrounds" from scratch. Then it'd be someone else's turn to verify *his* information.

His employer remained a mystery to him. They claimed to be a private security agency, and did accept security assignments for celebrities and high-risk government and corporate officials. That wasn't the bulk of their work. Sam still had no idea of the extent of their global operations, and something told him it wouldn't be smart to go digging for that information. He'd be "read in" on all that when the time came.

What he did know was that the types of missions his employer undertook were often incredibly dangerous and worth the inherent risks. His boss, Crispin Wilder, was a man of his word and did not throw his people under a bus when the shit hit the fan. That mattered.

Out of habit, as Sam walked he cataloged the "feel" of the city. Atlanta had a different rhythm from Chicago, which felt different from New York, LA, or Denver. It was one of his talents—getting a sense of a place, or of a person, finding the hidden things, be it personal or corporate. Some of it was uncanny intuition; most of it was being people savvy.

He nodded at a couple passing him on the street. They were dressed up, he in a suit and she in a pretty green cocktail dress. They held hands, smiling at each other as if there was no one else in the world. Sam did a quick ring check and wasn't surprised to see she wore a shiny diamond on her left hand. Probably recently engaged, if he read the vibes correctly.

They were lucky, as was this city. The month before, Atlanta had been in the crosshairs of a domestic terrorist looking to make his mark on history. Luckily, Quinton Ellers had never made it out of the South Georgia swamp with his ricin and military-grade explosives. Veritas had played a major role in stopping him, but the public was unaware of that. It was what Sam's boss preferred—do the dangerous stuff and let someone else take the credit. Yet another reason he wanted to work with Veritas on a full-time basis: They kicked ass.

He'd missed out on the swamp mission, playing tourist in Mexico. Looking back, he'd realized it'd been a test on Veritas's part: Did he have the moxie to handle an assignment on his own? After checking in at a fancy resort, he'd quickly identified which of the employees had been stashing heroin in the guest's luggage, using them as unsuspecting mules across the border.

Four Americans and two Brits were in the process of being released from Mexican jails because of his investigation, all charges dropped. Veritas's offer of a full-time job came right after that, and he'd jumped on it. Then celebrated by taking a real vacation, the first in years.

As Sam paused at an intersection a taxi rolled by, a lone Black woman in the back. For a moment, she looked over at him as they passed, and he swore he saw fear. No, maybe he'd imagined it. Suddenly eager to be back in his hotel room, he pushed his pace. Cutting down a side street to avoid the traffic, he skirted a drunk weaving along singing to himself.

Sam was about to cross the street to access the backside of his hotel when the same taxi rolled past him. The woman in the back was gesturing now, appearing upset about something. Probably the driver trying to pad the fare, telling her he couldn't find the address. That wouldn't surprise Sam since too many streets in this city shared the same name.

After he crossed the street, he was just about to walk around the gate arm that secured the parking lot when something made him pause. The taxi now idled at the curb near the entrance to an alley halfway down the block. It was an odd place to drop a fare, especially a young woman on her own.

Though tired and eager for a hot shower and bed, something about this scene bothered him. He scanned the street out of habit. There were no offices or apartments on that side, only the alley and a big parking lot with spotty security lighting. Was the cabbie dropping her off so she could claim her car?

A man exited the alley, heading straight for the cab. He was white, about six foot, dressed in jeans with a light-gray jacket and shaggy blond hair that touched his collar.

His left hand was stuck inside the jacket's pocket. Sam's cop instincts had him on the move even before the guy yanked open the rear door. The man shouted something to the passenger, gun drawn.

"Hey you! Get away from there!" Sam yelled.

Ignoring him, the assailant shouted again as the woman shook her head, frantically trying to crawl out the other side of the cab. Shots echoed in the night air.

"No! Stop!" Sam bellowed, his feet pounding across the pavement even though he was unarmed.

Reaching inside the cab, the gunman grabbed the woman's purse and then bolted down the alley in the semi-darkness. When Sam skidded to a halt near the side of the vehicle, he saw the blood spatter on the driver-side door. One glance inside told him the cabbie had earned his last fare. Opening the back door, Sam swore. The passenger's blouse was no longer white now, but flooding with red. Her mouth moved, trying to form words. Her stomach was rounded in pregnancy.

"Oh, God, no!"

He punched in 911 on his phone, then knelt beside the open door as he relayed the information to the operator in crisp tones. Pushing his phone back into his pocket, he leaned closer. The woman reached out for him, still trying to talk. He did a quick injury assessment, and from the rasping sound that came with each breath, he knew exactly what had happened: She'd taken a round in a lung.

Carefully pulling her free from the cab, he laid the injured woman on the ground, stripped off his jacket, rolled it up, and put it under her feet. He hoped the slight elevation might help as she grew increasingly shocky. With an apology, he ripped open her blouse, revealing a single wound on her left side, just below her bra. Blood bubbled from it with each inhalation and exhalation. Laying his palm over it, he felt the faint suction.

"Shit," he muttered. He knew this kind of injury all too well. You had to fight for each increasingly shallow breath, and it hurt like a son of a bitch.

He patted his pockets, but came up with nothing that would help seal the wound until the paramedics arrived. A quick search of the bloody cab located the remains of the driver's supper tucked under the front passenger seat, a meal that had included an empty plastic sandwich bag.

Good enough.

He quickly returned to the wounded woman, whose respirations were becoming increasingly labored. Her lips grew faintly blue as each breath pulled air through the wound and into the chest cavity, compressing her lungs. Suffocating her.

"Sorry, this is going to hurt, but it should help you breathe." He flattened out the plastic bag and placed it on top of the wound. Then pressed on it, hard, because he had no tape to seal it in place. The woman responded with a moan of deepest pain.

"The paramedics will be here really soon. You hang in there. I've been hurt like this and I survived. You and your little one will too."

As time passed, her breathing seemed to grow less labored, and that gave him some hope she might survive.

With his free hand Sam took hold of hers, squeezing it as her eyes narrowed in pain. "I'm sorry," he said. "I'm so sorry." If he'd been quicker, maybe scared the robber off . . .

"My baby . . . " she whispered. Blood dribbled from the corner of her mouth as a single tear threaded its way down a smooth cheek.

"Your baby will be fine. Just focus on taking each breath slowly. That's it. You're doing good. Slow and steady." Sirens came closer now. "They're almost here. Just breathe nice and slow."

Even as he pressed against her chest, willing her and the child to live, the woman clutched his free hand, bloody white fingers entwined with trembling black ones. Sam was still holding tight and praying when the paramedics arrived.

Hotel Rosemont
Tuesday, May 12th
2:11 a.m.

It was past two in the morning when Sam finally reached his hotel, emotionally shot. As he entered the lobby, the shocked expression on the desk clerk's face told him he looked like hell.

"Sir?" the woman asked, as her hand reached for the phone. "Are you okay?"

"I'm good," he said. Uninjured at least.

He walked over to the desk, displayed his room card, and gave his name. Once the clerk was assured he belonged there, he waved off her concerns and headed to his room.

It wasn't until Sam was inside the elevator that he saw himself as she had. Some moron had decided that it would look stylish if three of its walls were mirrored. Probably a fine idea if you were headed to a business meeting and wanted to check if your tie was crooked. But for Sam, the three reflections of his face brought home just how bad this night had been.

His usually bright brown eyes had that hollowed-out look, his light-brown hair went every which way, and his tanned face was pale and stubbled. Blood had spattered his shirt as he'd fought for every breath right along with the victim.

Too many memories.

The cops had found the woman's purse in the alley, cash, credit cards, and phone long gone. Her driver's license told them she was Treina Wilson, twenty-six, a local who lived in Midtown Atlanta. At least she had a name now.

While he'd spent time at the police station giving his statement, Ms. Wilson—Treina—had undergone surgery to fix the hole in her lung and a one-way valve had been inserted that allowed the trapped air to be expelled with each inhalation.

Because she was pregnant, she was in "guarded" condition, having lost a lot of blood into her chest cavity. The doctors had sedated her and intended to keep her that way until the lung was in better shape. But for now, both she and the baby were alive, and that was the best news of the whole damned nightmare.

It took some time, but Sam had been eliminated as a suspect. It probably would have taken longer if he'd fired his weapon, but he'd left it in the hotel safe since he'd spent the day sightseeing. Now he regretted that.

The homicide detectives had made him rehash his testimony over and over. You did that kind of thing in their job because sometimes the answers would change. He had no complaints with how Detectives Hall and Jones had handled his interview. When he'd asked why the victim had been driven to that particular location, they didn't know. It didn't make much sense, as Ms. Wilson's apartment was only ten minutes away from the crime scene, just to the north.

A glance at the clock on the nightstand told Sam he'd been staring at nothing for too long. He needed a shower, then sleep, but first there was the required phone call to Chicago.

If one of Veritas's employees was in any sort of situation that required interaction with law enforcement—even something as minor as a traffic ticket—company policy required them to report that incident promptly. It had seemed like a lot of handholding to Sam, but Veritas had its reasons, and its enemies, who'd love nothing more than to jack around with one of its people. Sometimes that jacking around resulted in being thrown in a Third World prison, where your only survival was contingent upon someone on the outside raising holy hell.

It was answered on the second ring. "It's Sam Marsh. I'm reporting a personal incident. I'm not currently on assignment."

"Are you in need of a lawyer or medical assistance?" a young man's voice asked. He sounded remarkably awake for the time of night, even if it was an hour earlier for him.

"No, I'm good," Sam replied. "I was a witness to a murder

and armed robbery."

There was a pause now. "Let me start recording. My name's Philip, by the way. I only work the night shift and that's why we've never met."

"Thank you, Philip. You ready?" Sam asked.

"I am."

He spent the next few minutes laying out the crime, how he happened to witness it, how the local cops didn't consider him a suspect, at least not yet.

"Anything else you need to tell us?" Philip asked. His accent hailed from somewhere in the upper Northeast, Maine maybe.

"No. If the cops start hassling me, I'll call it in."

"I'll make sure this is flagged for the proper people. If you need anything, let us know."

"I will. Thanks."

"Goodnight, Mr. Marsh."

As Sam disconnected the call, he spied the large patch of dried blood on his shirt, which explained the panicked stare he'd received from the front desk clerk. He ripped it off and tossed it in the wastebasket.

By now, the robber was probably flying high on drugs bought from the money he'd stolen, all because Treina Wilson had been in the wrong place at the wrong time.

Chapter Two

Hotel Rosemont
Tuesday, May 12th
5:50 a.m.

The knocks on Sam's door jarred him out of what promised to be a bad dream. He could always tell which ones those would be as they usually began with someone screaming and ended in blood. In this case, Treina Wilson was the one doing the screaming, and he the bleeding.

When he didn't immediately respond, the knocking resumed, louder now. It appeared that his day was about to start even when he didn't want it to. After pulling on a pair of jeans, he shuffled to the door and peered through the security peephole. On the other side was a woman wearing a dark-blue pantsuit, her light-brown hair in a tight bun. No earrings, no makeup. She looked as tired as he felt.

Opening the door, he stared at her. "Sorry, you have the wrong room."

"You're Samuel Marsh, right?" He nodded. "Then I don't have the wrong room." She raised a black wallet that contained a badge and an ID, let it hang in the air for all of three seconds, and then closed it. "Special Agent Driscoll, FBI. I need to talk to you about the shooting last night."

Sam's eyes were fully open now, his brain coming back online. That three-letter acronym starting with "F" did it every time. What the hell did the feds have to do with Treina Wilson's shooting?

"Let me see the ID again."

With an irritated frown, she held it up so he could confirm that it was genuine. Groaning, he waved her in knowing this conversation was going to require yet another call to Veritas. After clicking on the overhead light, which made him blink, Sam settled on the side of his bed.

The woman sat in his desk chair, moving right in, letting him know that she was in charge. He knew the drill, had played the same game countless times. It didn't intimidate him in the least.

"What does the FBI have to do with an armed robbery and murder? Is Ms. Wilson one of yours?"

A brusque shake of the head. "I need to know exactly how this went down. I want you to start from the moment you first had contact with . . . the victim."

The hesitation cleared the final cobwebs out of Sam's brain. Now that he studied Agent Driscoll he noticed that both her suit and her shirt were wrinkled, as if she'd grabbed the first one she could find. This wasn't the usual FBI drill. Those people always looked like they'd just gotten their clothes back from the cleaners.

There was also a pallor to her complexion, which made her caramel-brown eyes stand out even more. Those eyes were red rimmed and almost as hollow as his had been a few hours earlier.

"Mr. Marsh?" she nudged.

He really wasn't in the mood. "Read the police report, Agent Driscoll."

"I need to hear what happened in your own words."

Everything about this felt wrong. "Until you tell me why you're interested in this case, I'm not going to be helpful."

"Do you understand what kind of hell I can put you through if you refuse to answer my questions?" she demanded, her right hand bunched in a fist.

His instincts were correct: This was somehow personal. But until she leveled with him, he was just going to be a prick.

"Yeah, I know what you can do. I used to be a homicide

detective in Chicago, so I've worked cases with the Bureau before. The question remains: Why are you interested in *this* one? If I don't get an answer I like, I'll be calling your boss next."

It was purely a bluff, but the woman's face turned crimson. "Who the fuck do you think you are?"

Her reaction pushed his own surly button. "Right back at you, lady. You're the one pounding on my door at the crack of dawn."

Her breaths came in short puffs now. His challenge should have just backed her off, reminded her to be civil, not hit a nerve. But it had. Maybe head butting wasn't going to get either of them anywhere.

With a sigh, he decided to offer an olive branch. "Look, I'm tired and last night completely sucked. So just talk to me, one law-enforcement pro to another."

Agent Driscoll heaved a lengthy sigh, one that matched his. In a move he hadn't expected, she reached up, undid the bun at the back of her neck, then combed through it with her fingers. Her eyes weren't meeting his now. A few twists later, the hair was back in place. The move made her seem more human, perhaps a bit vulnerable. It had also allowed her to buy time before answering.

"Treina Wilson's mom is a dear friend of my mother's," she said, her eyes rising to his now. "They work together."

"This isn't a sanctioned FBI investigation then."

"No. This is my mother begging me to find out why Treina and her baby nearly died last night." She hesitated. "I heard what you did for her. Treina's still alive because of you. The family is *very* grateful. So is mine."

Sam accepted her olive branch in return. "We got lucky." He rubbed his face in weariness. "This is personal for you. I've been there, too." He needed more sleep, some coffee, and food, in that order. From the determined expression on the agent's face, only the latter two were going to be an option.

"Give me ten minutes and I'll meet you in the lobby," he said. "You buy me breakfast with as much coffee as I can possibly drink, and I'll tell you what went down. Then you're out of my hair."

Special Agent Driscoll opened her mouth as if to argue, then closed it. "Ten minutes. You take off on me and I'll hunt you down."

Another button pushed. "Really?" he said, shaking his head. "After I told you I used to work homicide, you think I'm going to bail on you?"

The woman opened the door now, frowning back at him. "You might. Because you're not a homicide cop anymore, and that makes me wonder why." She glanced down at her phone. "Nine and a half minutes. The clock is running, buddy."

As the door closed behind her, he resisted the urge to flip her off. Unfortunately, despite her crappy attitude, the only way to get this surly fed out of his hair was to tell her what he knew.

Yeah, that went well.

Susan rolled her eyes as she paced back and forth in front of the gas fireplace in the front lobby. Unfortunately, her pacing had drawn the notice of the front desk clerk who looked like she was about to place a phone call to the cops. Susan shot her a "mind your own business" frown, then continued pacing.

Her mom's panicked phone call had come during one of the few times she'd been asleep tonight. Not that her mother knew Susan was suffering from intermittent insomnia. If she had known, the family would intervene, mostly in the form of solicitous visits, numerous phone calls, and insistent worrying. Susan certainly wasn't up for any of that right now.

She'd hoped to scam the police report out of the investigating detectives, and had been happy to find that one of them was her ex-boyfriend. No such luck; Pat Hall had told her it wasn't her case and to go the hell home and get some sleep. At least she'd gotten Marsh's name and where he was staying in the city, which had landed her in the man's hotel room before dawn.

Once they'd seen her badge, the average citizen would have freaked and told her everything she wanted to know. Not this guy. Right off, he'd figured out she was doing a solo thing, which meant he was too damned perceptive.

Susan sank onto one of the chairs near the fireplace, rubbing her eyes. She'd met her mom at the hospital earlier, spent time with Treina's family while she was in surgery, felt the fear that they'd lose both her and the baby. Even now, her mom was still there with Mama Wilson and the others, holding hands, whispering prayers, and sending text updates.

But one key person had been missing—the baby's father. When Susan had asked about him, the answers had been vague. Something about how the family hadn't met him yet, and didn't even know his name, even though Treina had said he'd asked her to marry him and she'd agreed. That had made Susan suspicious, but she'd held her questions because it just wasn't the time for them. She knew she'd be conducting her own investigation soon enough.

Her mom's call had been the cap to a shitty day. Yet again, Susan had tangled with her boss, Special Agent in Charge Maxine Rhodes. It appeared the time off that Susan had been ordered to take—the word "suspension" had yet to be used—hadn't tempered her boss's attitude. Her relationship with Rhodes had always been rocky, but it'd definitely foundered in the last couple of weeks.

Susan's independent investigation of a militia group in South Georgia had resulted in preventing hundreds of deaths and injuries. The man the FBI had initially arrested in regard to the case was a former Army Ranger. Brannon Hardegree had eventually been released, all charges dropped, because he'd been instrumental in ensuring that the madman behind the planned attack never made it to Atlanta.

The official story was that Hardegree (who was never named in the news reports) had been working undercover for the D.C. Bureau office. Susan knew that to be utter bullshit, but a needed fiction because he'd actually been working undercover for an organization named Veritas. Unfortunately, with Quinton Ellers dead and Hardegree untouchable, that left her as the target of her boss's wrath.

Being blindsided by one of her own agents had made Rhodes furious. Susan seemed to have a talent for that, which was probably why she kept doing it. It was as if she had this need to piss off her boss, which only made her sound like a petulant teenager, rather than a seasoned FBI agent.

Yesterday another warning had been issued: If Susan kept up the solo-agent act she would be on suspension, pending a disciplinary hearing. Now here she was, already pushing the envelope. A sensible person would let the cops conduct their investigation, keep out of the way, but there was no chance that was going to happen, not after hearing her mother plead for her to help. If she had a choice of whom to disappoint, her boss or Rachel Driscoll, it sure as hell wouldn't be her mom.

Just as Susan was about to storm back upstairs and corral the ex-cop, the elevator dinged and Marsh appeared. He'd dressed in a crisp blue shirt, a black jacket, and the same worn jeans, which fit him perfectly. He had one of those youthful faces that made it difficult to judge his age correctly. At first glance, she'd have guessed him to be in his mid- to late twenties, but now she'd say a decade older. Thirty-five or thirty-seven maybe. Since he'd been a homicide detective, mid-thirties seemed about right. Her practiced eye noticed the slight bulge in his jacket on the right side. Probably a shoulder holster, which meant he was armed.

His hair had been combed and was sandy brown, his eyes a dark brown, and a light beard stubbled his face since he hadn't bothered to shave. He wasn't bulked up like some guys, but she could tell he worked out. He had too much muscle definition not to. He looked more like someone you'd find at an investment brokerage or standing behind a lectern at a university. Certainly not a cop. People probably dismissed him as young and inexperienced. She suspected that would be a mistake.

Marsh nodded at the front desk clerk, who continued to watch their every move, then angled his head toward the door.

Susan fell into step next to him.

"Before we eat, let's take a walk first," he said. "I want to retrace my steps from the moment I saw the victim in the cab."

He set a fast pace out the front door, no doubt figuring the sooner he showed her what she wanted, the quicker she'd leave him alone. They were in agreement on that.

"You visit the crime scene?" he asked.

"No, I came to talk to you first. It was too dark to see anything at that point."

They rounded the side of the hotel and headed toward the back. After negotiating their way through the employee parking lot, they walked around the gate. Once past the barrier, Sam came to a halt, staring down the road.

"It was just down there," he said, pointing. By now, the crime scene had been processed, the cabbie's body had been removed, the taxi towed. As if it had never happened.

When she started that way, Marsh touched her arm, angling his head the other direction. "Let's start from the beginning."

"What do you mean?"

"I first saw her in the cab a few blocks from here. Let's start there and work back."

Susan didn't see the point, but since he didn't act as if he was going to change his mind, she gave in. Once across the street, they headed north, then took a left at the first side street.

"How well do you know Treina?" he asked.

"Not very well. Her mom works with mine at the Atlanta Community Food Bank. They've grown close over the years. I've met Treina at a couple family get-togethers."

"Okay. Since we're going to be spending some time together, may I call you Susan?" he asked.

"No, Driscoll works better."

"Driscoll it is. So much for adding you to my Christmas card list," he replied.

Susan frowned over at him. "Were you in a cab or on foot when you saw Treina?"

"On foot. I like to walk. I learn more that way."

"Why take the side streets?" she asked. It seemed like the

kind of thing a local would do, not a tourist.

"I like to scout around, get a sense of the place, see what I can find out about any city I visit. Did you know there's a Santeria and Voodoo shop south of downtown?"

She did, because she'd had a case involving the former. "Yeah, I've been in there."

"Cool store. I bought my sister a mojo bag. She's into that kind of thing."

"And this is relevant . . . why?"

"It's not, but it is relevant to the city's culture, and that sometimes can be important." He looked over at her now. "When I was out walking, I found this hole-in-the-wall Mexican place with the most remarkable *carne asada.*"

She heard the awe in his tone. "Oh, God, you're a foodie."

"A what?"

"One of those people who will canoe down the Amazon just to find some exotic dish that no one else has ever tasted, preferably one with bugs in it."

Marsh slowed his pace, a smile forming on his face. "Well, maybe, except the bug thing. Don't you like to eat?"

"I do, but I don't worship food." In fact, she hadn't been eating much at all, not since her time in the swamp.

He shook his head. "That's sad. I bet you've never had Chicago-style pizza."

"Pizza is pizza."

He gave her a shocked look that spoke of deepest pity. "That'd be like saying collard greens are just a bunch of weeds."

She shuddered at that. "Okay, but you're still a foodie."

They went one more block, and then he halted and pointed at the intersection.

"For me, it all started here."

6:30 a.m.

By the time they returned to the crime scene, Susan had her head filled with details. Samuel Marsh, the ex-homicide detective from the Windy City, now a licensed private investigator, had seen things that most people wouldn't have noticed. At least not when they were on vacation. Like the fact that Treina had seemed afraid even before the cab had stopped. How she'd become agitated when it had pulled over on this poorly lit section of the street.

"I want to know why the cabbie stopped *here*," Marsh said, standing close to a dark stain on the street, the remnants of the blood that had been hosed down once the crime-scene folks were finished. "Unless she was going to pick up her car, it makes no sense."

Susan let her gaze drift over to the closest lot, the one across from the rear of the hotel. "You think her ride's here somewhere?" Even before he could formulate an answer, she typed out a text. "I'm asking her sister about the car."

Marsh nodded. "Any word on how Treina's doing?"

Susan didn't call him on using the victim's first name. If you'd been the one to keep her alive until the paramedics arrived, you had that right.

"My last update from my mother said she's still in guarded condition. They're keeping her sedated. So far the baby is staying put."

"Thank God," he said.

She looked up from the phone, seeing the stark relief on his face. She could imagine what it'd been like to watch as Treina struggled for her next breath. "Your first aid made all the difference. How did you learn to handle a sucking chest wound?"

Marsh didn't reply, but instead turned away and walked down the alley, searching the ground with methodical precision. The scene had already been worked over by the forensics team, but Mr. Chicago seemed to think he'd find something else. She also noted he had skillfully avoided answering her question.

I wonder why.

Susan's phone pinged. She sent follow-up questions and then hurried to catch up with Marsh. "According to Treina's sister, her car is not at her apartment. It's a red Honda Hybrid and it has a bunged-up rear bumper. She didn't know the license-plate number." But she bet a quick call to Pat could obtain that, along with another lecture about staying out of his investigation.

"Well, at least the description will narrow it down," Marsh said, still scanning the ground.

"What are you looking for?"

"Don't know until I see it," was the curt reply. He kept searching until he reached the end of the alley. "Which way did you go?" he muttered.

For a second she was confused by the question, until she realized he was talking about the shooter. "What are you thinking, Marsh?"

He turned to her now, brows furrowed. "I'm thinking that our Ms. Wilson was brought to this location on purpose, and it wasn't her idea. Maybe it was just supposed to be a robbery, but somehow it went wrong."

"You're wasting time here. You haven't found anything that the cops missed."

Marsh arched an eyebrow. "It's my time to waste. Besides, you still owe me breakfast. I might as well earn it."

She resisted the urge to roll her eyes, and instead checked her e-mail while her companion continued to do his bloodhound imitation. It wasn't likely he'd find anything, but then she doubted the crime-scene techs had gone this far from the scene when they were collecting evidence.

There were no new messages, other than Joe Britelli's concerned e-mail wondering how she was doing on her "leave of absence." Apparently, he'd heard about her meeting with the boss. She made sure not to tell her partner exactly how she was courting a reprimand. It was bad enough that he was suggesting she see her doctor about the insomnia.

Susan joined the PI farther down the road, the one that led to the left from the T intersection. Marsh squatted, pointing at a broken brick, then pieces of pink plastic. "See that?"

"Yeah."

He rose and walked a few more feet, then pointed again. More pink plastic. Another twenty feet farther along, and this time, the plastic was mixed with what looked to be crushed electronics, the kind you'd find inside a smartphone.

"Huh." Susan took a picture with her cell phone for future reference, in case it actually turned out to be evidence. Pulling a pen from her purse, she bent down and carefully rolled over the largest piece, making sure not to touch it with her fingers. "It's a Samsung." She looked back at where the first pieces had been found, and it clicked. "The brick. He smashed it there and then dribbled it out as he ran."

"That's my guess. He could have made some bucks off that phone. Why destroy it?"

She shot off another text to Valeria. As she waited, she tapped a foot.

"You're hyperactive, aren't you?" he asked.

Her eyes flicked to him. "Yeah. I like to be on the move. My mom says I have the energy of a toddler. She should know: She babysits my sister's twins."

He nodded sagely, as if she'd just revealed an essential truth about herself.

"What?" she demanded. Her phone pinged before he could answer, and she read the message aloud. "Treina had a Samsung Galaxy and the case was hot pink."

They looked down at the remnants of both of those things.

"How the hell did you figure that out?" she asked.

Marsh shrugged. "I see stuff other people don't. Always been that way."

"Then you must have been a helluva homicide detective."

"Some might not agree," he said, and headed back the way they'd come.

Chapter Three

Alley near Hotel Rosemont
Tuesday, May 12th
8:15 a.m.

It'd taken another hour for a bored, middle-aged crime-scene tech to arrive, take photos of the debris in its various locations, then bag up the new evidence, the brick included. During all that time, Sam's stomach grumbled, reminding him that he needed food.

Still, the hour had been well spent. As they'd waited, they checked out all the cars in the parking lot and came up short of a red Honda with a damaged bumper. While they hunted, he found himself increasingly intrigued by Susan Driscoll.

She stood about five eight or so, his height, her hair a lighter shade of brown in the full sun, with those warm brown eyes. Her skin was tanned and the freckles that dotted her nose seemed at odds with her "I will kick you in the balls" attitude. Her body was lithe like a ballet dancer's, but with subtle curves that looked good on her. Everything about the woman told him Susan was smart—and tightly strung. His gut also told him something else was going on.

"Hey, Marsh?" she called out after she'd ended another call. "Stand where the cab was last night." He dutifully returned to the spot, wondering what she was up to, and watched as she headed into the alley.

"Don't think about taking off, Driscoll," he called out, nearly echoing her words to him earlier that morning. "You owe me breakfast," he added. No response. For a second, he wondered if she'd done just that. When she appeared again, Susan followed the exact path the robber had taken.

Her expression was pensive when she rejoined him. "The killer had to know the cab was going to be here. If not, he wouldn't have seen it until he came out from behind that sign."

"So he walks out, sees the woman is on her own, decides she'd be a perfect victim? And does all that in a split second? I don't know. If I were him, I'd have waited until she was out of the cab and it had rolled off. A female on her own at night? Tempting target. But why go after her when she was still inside the vehicle and there was a witness?"

"Maybe he thought she'd just been picked up, and he was about to lose his chance," Susan countered.

"Okay. What if the cabbie was in on the robbery?" He shook his head immediately. "If he was, why shoot him?"

"The robber didn't want to split the loot?" she suggested.

He raised an eyebrow at that. "Possible." His stomach rumbled again, loudly. "Look, you need to feed me. That was our agreement, right?"

The frown appeared instantly, then slowly vanished. "Okay, let's get you fed. Can't have it said a Southerner didn't treat a Yankee right."

"You're a local?" he asked.

"Born and bred. I'm a true Georgia peach," she said, upping her light Southern accent and adding in a dazzling smile now. A couple of cute dimples had formed, and her eyes seemed less weary. He found he liked all that, even if he knew the smile to be forced. Maybe this was how she really was when she wasn't so stressed.

"Me? I'm a Chicagoan, through and through. Couldn't be more of a Yankee if I tried."

"I'm *so* sorry," she said. "Not all of us are as blessed as I am."

His laughter broke free. "Just a matter of perspective."

"Yes, it is." She paused, then added, "I better drive."

"Please do. You know, I don't get it. Atlanta had a big fire just like Chicago, and instead of taking that opportunity to carefully lay out your streets in a sensible grid pattern, you just let them go any which way. Then you insist on changing street names whenever it suits you. I got lost *three* times the other day, and I was using a damned GPS."

She eyed him. "It's good to keep you Northerners confused. Should have done it before Sherman came to call. Hey, at least my town got torched because of a war. Yours was because of a clumsy cow."

He opened his mouth to argue, then snapped it shut.

"Gotcha."

Then she burst out laughing, and for a fraction of a second he spied the real woman beneath the plain-Jane suit.

Babs Midtown
9:00 a.m.

Susan took him to a place called Babs, where she ordered a bagel with smoked salmon and he went for the spinach, goat cheese, and grilled Portobello omelet with a double side order of pork sausage.

"Foodie," she muttered, pointing her fork at his plate. When he didn't rise to the bait, she took a long sip of her coffee. No surprise, it was black.

"How long have you been with the FBI?" he asked.

"Eight years. All of them here in Atlanta."

"Married?" She shook her head. "Dating?"

"Next question," she said, though she didn't seem upset by the last one.

"Then tell me what Treina does for a living."

"She's a paralegal, works for one of the biggest law firms in the city."

"Criminal or civil cases?"

"Both. The lawyer she works for handles high-profile civil cases."

"He straight arrow or a sleaze?"

There was a hint of a smile at his question. "Very straight arrow, from what I gather. The firm's other two partners handle the criminal cases and they're sleazes. Edward Mossman is a slime ball in a two-thousand-dollar suit. Charles Warburg Sr. is old Southern money, used to handing out bribes and backslapping with the good ol' boys."

"I take it you've tangled with these guys."

"No, but our office has. We spent over a year building a case against a local businessman. Had him dead to rights on bribery, extortion, you name it. We were going to RICO his ass."

Sam whistled under his breath. If the FBI had accrued enough evidence to go for federal charges under the Racketeer Influenced and Corrupt Organizations Act, that had to have been a major case.

"We get within a few weeks of trial and witnesses start recanting their testimonies, or disappearing. As in, *never seen again*. We were hosed. We never did figure out how it all fell apart, but his lawyers had inside help, that was for certain."

"Inside the FBI?"

"No, the police department, we think. Not sure on that."

Once Sam had finished off his plate, then his latte, he wondered if he should order more of both. He was that hungry. Instead, he pushed his plate away. Maybe he'd score an early lunch in an hour or so.

Her phone rang. "Driscoll. Oh, hi Valeria." She mouthed *Treina's sister*, then walked away for privacy. As he watched Susan's expression, praying this wasn't bad news, he realized he owed Veritas a phone call. Might as well get it over with.

Sam dialed the number. "It's Marsh."

"Hello, Sam," Sanjay replied. He handled the majority of Veritas's mission-related calls, at least during the day. "Anything new since early this morning?"

"I'm not on a mission, so is there someone else I should be talking to rather than taking up your time?"

"No, the moment the word 'murder' landed in your report,

you got bumped to my oversight."

"Okay." How the guy kept up with everything, Sam had no idea. "Yes, there is something new." He lowered his voice, though Susan was still on the other call. "This morning I was rousted out of bed by an FBI agent who wanted to know all about the shooting. Her name is Susan Driscoll, and from what I can tell, this isn't an official investigation. She's a friend of the family."

"Driscoll? Well, you're in luck. Brannon worked with her. She's the agent who helped him stop that terrorist from attacking Atlanta."

Sam's eyes tracked to the woman where she stood by one of the windows. The sunlight backlit her hair, causing it to shine.

"Really? Small world, isn't it?" he said.

"Very. Brannon had nothing but respect for the lady, which should tell you something."

"It does." Anyone the former Army Ranger respected was the real deal. Maybe that was good news, because Sam was sitting on the fence about whether he was going to help her with this case or not. "What's Veritas's policy about me conducting an investigation on my own time?"

"You know, you just cost me ten bucks. Morgan said you'd ask that question. I figured with you being on vacation, you wouldn't."

"Sorry." Morgan Blake was an ex-FBI agent, now with Veritas. She'd know where his head was at the moment. "So what's the answer?"

"Our boss has no issues with it. He's aware of what happened last night and figured you might be interested in following this through. He said he trusts your instincts."

So Sam had Veritas's approval if he wanted to move forward. A quick look at the now-pacing agent told him Susan might be the problem.

"What's our relationship with the Atlanta FBI office?"

"Frosty, at best. D.C. likes us, but the boss lady in Atlanta does not. So watch your step."

"Got it. Can you update my incident report for me?"

"Sure will. How was the rest of your vacation?"

"Really good." *Until last night.* "Looking forward to being in the office on Monday."

"We're looking forward to having you around all the time. We love harassing the newbies."

"Hah. No way you can beat the hazing at the CPD."

"Who do you think taught them all they know?" Sanjay retorted. "We'll see you Monday."

"Thanks, Sanjay. Bye."

Susan returned to the table shortly after he put his phone away, her expression guarded.

"Anything new?" he asked.

She shook her head, which told him there was and that she wasn't willing to share.

"I'm going to talk to Treina's family again, see what I can find out about her fiancé." At Sam's puzzled look, she added. "Yeah, she's engaged. But he still hasn't made an appearance, and that bugs me. If I can find him, maybe he'd know why she was taking a cab instead of using her own car."

"Good plan." Sam scooped up the check at her protest. "I'll take care of this, in trade for something."

"Which is?"

"I want to work case with you."

"No."

"I have a stake in it. You *know* I do."

"No, you don't. Not to be harsh, but you were merely a bystander, a good Samaritan. Your part is done."

"That's a real pot-and-kettle argument, Agent Driscoll. Your friends would be planning a funeral if I hadn't been at the scene."

She winced at the brutal truth. "I got that. But no matter what, you're not part of this investigation. Go visit another museum, or get on a plane and go home. Doesn't matter to me. You keeping sticking your nose into this and I'll make sure you get a firsthand tour of one of our city's finest jail cells."

Sam registered the stubbornness in her eyes. Arguing would

get him nowhere. So he gave her a nod, as if he'd acquiesced, knowing that wasn't the case. And just to be a gentleman, he picked up the check.

Tempted as she'd been to let Marsh find his own way back to the hotel, she'd offered to give him a ride anyway. She'd expected him to fluff up, get hostile when she told him to back off. He hadn't. That told her she'd either won that round, or he was ignoring her. Her good instincts said it was the latter, because that's exactly what she would do.

Despite the fact that she didn't want him in the way, Samuel Marsh was observant, quick on the uptake, methodical. He also wasn't telling her everything. It was time to do some digging.

"Do you own your own PI firm, or work for someone else?"

"I worked solo after I left the CPD, and I also did freelance work for another firm. Starting Monday, I'll be full-time with them."

"What firm is that?"

He looked over. "Veritas. I suspect you've heard of them."

The car swerved for a fraction of a second as she adjusted to that news. "You're kidding me."

"No. I phoned them while you were talking to Treina's sister. I'm required to notify them if I have any contact with a law-enforcement officer. In this case, you."

"Then you know everything that happened in the swamp?"

"Other than the fact that Veritas thinks you're a helluva federal agent, that's about it. I haven't had a chance to read the full mission report yet." He looked over at her now. "Is it true you're on the outs with your boss because of us?"

It would be easy to claim that, but it wasn't entirely true. "Not completely. Agent Rhodes and I have been tangling since the day she replaced my old boss. He was great. She's all about the rule book."

"While you're all about solving cases, right?"

She frowned over at him now. "And you aren't?"

"Touché," he said. "I also know that sometimes you have to feed the dragon a tidbit or two to keep it from eating you."

She ground her teeth and then remembered what her dentist had said about that. Even *he* was getting on her case.

"Sometimes butting heads is a waste of time," he added. "It's all about power, and if she thinks you're not keeping her in the loop, she'll get spooked. Some bosses are just that way."

"Been there, done that?" she asked, parroting his words.

A nod returned. "Is that why you aren't a homicide detective now?"

"No. I'm not a cop because I didn't trust my instincts. Sometimes, that mistake can cost you everything."

They parted at the front of the hotel.

"Stay out of trouble, Chicago," Susan said.

Sam could tell he was already in her rearview, her mind skipping ahead to the tasks she needed to do once he was out of her hair.

"Oh, I'll stay out of trouble, no problem there," he replied, smiling over at her. "Have a good day. I know we'll be seeing each other again." He shut the car door before she could reply and issued a jaunty wave as he disappeared inside the front doors.

No way was he backing off now. He'd be sure to stay out of the APD's way, but as an outsider he'd see things the local cops might not notice. Or at least that was his way of justifying his part in all this. Truth was, holding that pregnant woman and praying she wouldn't die had somehow made him feel responsible for justice being served. He wanted her shooter in shackles, shuffling into court, head bowed, knowing he was facing death row. It was a matter of honor now.

Of course, his decision to continue snooping on his own would put him in conflict with Susan. He'd have to find a way to work around that obstacle, because she sure as hell wasn't backing down.

Susan reminded him of his former partner, Keith. Keith had been hard-charging, not holding back, pushing to clear cases, hustling through life as if the job was the only thing that mattered. Because it was to him. He'd been divorced, no kids, no reasons not to put in the long hours.

Sam had worked the hours, done his job, but he'd also made sure to take time to stroll along the lakeshore at dawn if possible. He'd attended concerts, gone for walks in Jackson Park. He'd savored each day as if it were his last, because if he hadn't, the job would have killed him long before it did his partner.

Magnolia Cab Company
Noon

After he'd showered, Sam surfed the news reports until he found the address of the cab company. From what he could tell, it wasn't one of the major taxi companies in the city. As he drove to the destination, he realized how much he missed his home. Here, there was no "L" rattling down the street, no Chicago vibe. Susan could easily tell him about all the wonderful things Atlanta had to offer, and they'd all be true. But it still wasn't home.

The Magnolia Cab Company's office was in an old wooden building that looked to have been built about the turn of the century. That made sense, as not many of Atlanta's structures had survived General Sherman's parting "bonfire" in 1864. This building's windows appeared to be the originals, but the metal grills covering them looked fairly new, a hint that even a cab company was fair game for burglars.

Sam pushed open the door and found himself in a room full of blue-gray cigarette smoke that would have made a tobacco farmer proud. His eyes and nose immediately complained about the abuse. Someone had tacked a "No Smoking" sign to a messy bulletin board, but it too was smoke stained. At one time, Chicago's police stations had been like this.

The place was empty but for two men who sat in the back, working the phones and computer screens, tracking cabs all over the city. An old wooden counter delineated the space between Sam and them, which meant this place had once served a business with walk-in traffic. Now, that counter was littered with stacks of paper, used Styrofoam coffee cups, and a full ashtray. After the closest dispatcher sent a cab to the Amtrak station, he headed toward him.

"Need a cab?" the man asked. He was painfully scrawny, probably because of the cigarette hanging out of his mouth.

"No, I need information." Sam slid a ten across the top of the counter, avoiding the ashtray.

The man scooped up the bill. "Whaddya need to know?"

"Arnie Myers, the cab driver who was shot last night? I need to know where he picked up his fare." Since that detail wasn't available from the victim.

"Arnie picked that fare up at Atlantic Station."

The answer came too quickly. "You don't have to look that up?"

"No. A cop asked me the same thing."

One of Atlanta's finest was earning their keep. "Did the fare call in to request a cab?"

"No. Sometimes the drivers just roll around and pick up fares on their own if it's a slow night."

"Would you have the cabbie's home address?"

The dispatcher looked down at the counter again, then back up. "Depends."

Sam got the hint and forked over another ten, and it vanished like the first one.

"Yeah, I got it."

The dispatcher pulled over a stained piece of paper, a receipt of some kind, and scribbled out the address. "Everybody wants to know about Arnie today."

As Sam accepted the piece of paper, he asked, "Someone besides the cop?"

"Yeah. Had a guy in here first thing this morning asking the same thing."

"What did this guy look like?"

As the dispatcher spun out the description, Sam felt his pulse pick up; it matched last night's shooter. "You got security cameras in here?"

"Are you kidding? I heard the SBH got hurt too. That's a shame," the dispatcher added.

"SBH?"

"Single Black hottie. We've got a code we use for the fares. BOB for bitchy old broad. DFB for drunk frat boy. Things like that. Makes the time go faster."

"Never knew that. Thanks. You've been a big help."

The guy shrugged and returned to his work, twenty bucks richer for less than a minute's work, and apparently not too bummed about Arnie's death.

Chapter Four

Arnie Myers's Apartment
12:30 p.m.

Sam's burst of optimism withered as he turned onto the block where Arnie Myers had lived. In front of the rundown apartment complex was a nest of cop cars, and parked nearby was a medical examiner's van. It didn't take a genius to know someone had died here and that the cab driver's building was now a crime scene.

"Dammit," he muttered.

This was too much like his old job. Except, back in the day and on his home turf, he could have signed in, hoofed it up to the apartment and ducked under the crime-scene tape. Now, as a private citizen, he had to resort to loitering near a pair of uniformed cops, eavesdropping like everyone else.

As he waited like a morbid gawker, he learned how the Atlanta Braves had done during their last home game, and that one of the cops was banging a nurse at Grady Hospital. It was only when a third officer joined them that Sam got what he needed: Might be a robbery gone bad, the newcomer said. Victim all beaten to hell, and the apartment tossed.

"Huh. Probably a junkie," one of the cops said.

"Yeah, well, this junkie was stupid. He tore the place apart, but left behind some meth and a bunch of pills in one of the bedroom drawers. One thing's for sure, he's a mean bastard. Tortured the hell out of the vic. I about puked when I first saw the body."

Tortured? Did this have anything to do with Treina's shooting?

He glanced up to see one of the detectives who'd interviewed him the night before exit the building. Sam waited until Patrick Hall headed toward a car, then hurried to catch up with him, hoping to have a few words.

As he approached, the cop turned on instinct. Hall was probably in his early forties, still physically fit, but the long hours and the inevitable crappy diet was beginning to show around his middle. His blond hair needed a trim, but his eyes were sharp and focused on Sam.

"Marsh? What are you doing here?"

"Being nosy," he said.

"Why? This isn't Chicago, and this isn't your case."

Sam smiled. "You did a background check on me," he said, not surprised. It's exactly what he would have done.

Hall nodded. "Yeah, I wonder why it is a guy who used to work homicide failed to mention that little detail last night."

"It wasn't germane to the case."

The detective raised an eyebrow as if he thought that was bullshit. "So how'd we do?" he asked.

He meant in terms of the interview. "You asked every question I would have."

"I know," Hall said, nodding. "Just wanted to find out if you were going to be a dick about it, or not."

Sam laughed. He missed this kind of cop talk.

"So how'd you figure out the cabbie lived here?" Hall asked.

Sam told him what he'd learned from the dispatcher, how a man who'd been so interested in the dead guy's address matched the shooter from the night before.

The detective's eyes narrowed. "Give me a minute or two. Don't wander off. We need to have a chat."

Hall walked back to the building and went inside. Probably to talk to his partner so they could arrange for the cab company's dispatcher to do a session with a sketch artist.

When he returned, Hall asked, "You want to some coffee?"

"Sure. I could handle a cup." Because Sam knew that a detective in the first twenty-four hours of a murder investigation wouldn't be going for coffee with a witness unless he had a damned good reason.

"Then let's get out of here," Hall said. "Oh, and you're buying."

Emory University Hospital
12:45 p.m.

Only Valeria Wilson remained in the ICU's waiting room, and Susan took that as a good sign. If things were bad, the whole family would be here. Treina's older sister was tall and lean, with those sculpted cheekbones that fashion models loved. Today her face was gaunt, her eyes still red from the horrors of the night before. Her coal-black hair was pulled up in a tight bun on the back of her head, a colorful scarf securing it in place.

"Susan," the woman said, rising. They hugged.

"How's Treina doing?" Susan asked as they sat on two adjoining chairs.

"Better," Valeria replied. "They're still keeping her sedated to reduce the stress on the baby and to let her chest clear." Her voice was like rich coffee, still carrying traces of her birthplace in Jamaica.

"How's the baby doing?"

"Hanging in there. The little man is tough, that's for sure."

"A boy, huh?"

Valeria nodded. A frown appeared now. "Where the hell is his father?"

"Is it possible he doesn't know what happened to Treina?"

"Maybe. I have no idea. Tre's been really quiet about him. You can tell she's in love, but she won't say much." Valeria sighed. "She promised we'd meet him this coming weekend. It's my birthday and we're having a party. Tre promised to explain why they've been so secret about it all. She said we'd really like him because he's a good man."

And a very absent man. Susan wasn't sure what that meant. "Is it someone from her workplace, maybe?"

"I wondered that myself, but she said that the firm has a strict no-dating policy in place."

"Yeah, like that ever works." Valeria nodded her understanding. "Did Treina ever talk about anyone in particular? A friend maybe?"

"No. She said working there wasn't like at some of the other firms. She seemed more nervous the last few weeks, but I figured it was because she was pregnant. Oh, and a woman from the law firm was here earlier today. Sorry, I didn't get her name. She couldn't get in to see Tre, so she left."

"No problem." A visit to Warburg, Mossman and Day was needed, but with that came risks, at least to her career. "I'll find a way to check them out."

"Bless you," Valeria said, taking her hand. Then she broke out in tears. Susan pulled her in for another hug, because sometimes that was exactly what was needed most.

Starbucks
1:00 p.m.

They took Detective Hall's car to the closest coffee shop, a Starbucks of course. There seemed to be one on every second block in this city, and this one was inside a grocery store. Both of them ordered their coffee black, mostly because Sam didn't want the ribbing he'd get if he bought a latte. Not that the cop was being a hassle.

On the contrary, Hall was a quiet man, thoughtful, and in many ways reminded Sam of himself when he'd worn the badge. He also knew that the detective was sizing him up.

"You working this on your own, or with someone?" the man asked after they'd settled into a booth.

Sam saw no reason to avoid the question. "On my own at present, though there is someone else nosing around."

"Name?"

"Can't do that. The individual prefers to remain off everyone's radar at present."

Hall chewed on that, then sighed. "I knew Susan wouldn't back down."

Sam started in surprise.

The cop took a sip of his coffee, then set the cup down. "She showed up at the precinct, wanting to know details about the shooting. I sent her packing. I'm guessing she went after you next."

"Oh yeah. Nothing like having a pissed-off FBI agent pounding on your door before dawn."

Hall snorted. "That's her all right."

"I've shared what I've discovered so far. Are you willing to do the same?"

"Within reason," the man replied. "The dead body in the apartment is the cabbie's roommate, a Mr. Eric Bush. We ran a quick background check and he was clean. Which makes me wonder why was he beaten to death and the apartment tossed."

Sam leaned back in the bench seat. "Damned if I know. The suspect acted like it wasn't his first rodeo. He was at the cab, door open, and yelling at the victim even before I could get across the street. In fact, he didn't give her near enough time to hand over her purse. He just started shooting."

"Was he using?"

"It's possible. I never got close enough to him to be sure."

"Who was shot first? The woman or the driver?"

Sam closed his eyes and reran the scene in his mind. "My guess is the driver."

"To stop him from taking off?" Sam shrugged. "So we have one dead cabbie, one injured passenger, the cabbie's roommate beaten to a pulp, and his place tossed."

"Is it true the suspect left behind a stash?" Sam asked.

"Yes. How'd you find that out?"

"Overheard a couple street cops."

"So how'd you get hooked up with Veritas?"

Apparently the cop had been doing a lot of digging. "How did you find out I work for them?"

"Got a buddy at the CPD. I gave him a call last night. Speaks well of you."

"Huh. How familiar are you with Veritas?" Sam hedged.

Hall raised an eyebrow. "I've heard a few things. Word is that you folks did some damned good work down in South Georgia. *Unofficially*, of course. You have my sincere thanks for getting Suz out of that hellhole alive."

Apparently, whatever had gone on between Susan and this cop hadn't just been business.

"I'll pass the word on to Chicago."

"I'd appreciate that."

"I did some freelance work for them," Sam added. "I'm going full-time on Monday."

"I also heard they only hire the best," Hall said, watching for his reaction.

"We'll find out soon enough."

The detective downed the rest of his coffee, his way of indicating the interview was over. Sam did the same and followed him out the front door.

As they drove back to the crime scene, Hall asked, "How long were you with the Chicago PD?"

"Ten years. You?"

"Just passed my twelfth year."

Sam whistled. "You're a better man than me."

"Why'd you get out?"

He suspected the man already knew, but he answered the question anyway. "Lost a partner. Couldn't face it after that."

Hall gave him a long look and then went quiet, as if knowing any follow-up questions would not be appreciated. That silence lasted until the cop parked his car near the apartment complex. He turned off the engine, stared out the windshield for a time, then turned toward Sam.

"I have two options here: Tell you to stay the hell away from our investigation, or use your expertise in case you unearth something we don't. If I tell you to back off, will you catch the next plane home like a good little tourist?"

"Unlikely."

"Figured. I wouldn't either," Hall replied. "Then you do whatever it is you're gonna do, but be careful. If you get hurt or die, that's your problem. Well, unless you're dead and I end up with the case, which would really piss me off."

Sam grinned. "I'll do my best not to screw up your caseload."

"I'd appreciate that. In return for me turning a blind eye, you're going to promise not to fuck up my case."

"Not a problem. I know exactly how far I can push it."

"Good. And one final thing: If you end up working with Susan, watch her back. She gets the bit in her teeth and runs like she's at the Preakness. She's got great instincts, but sometimes she just needs someone there to slow her down." He paused. "Let me guess, she didn't give you her cell-phone number."

"No, in fact she threatened me with jail time if I kept poking around."

Hall laughed. "She's one helluva woman, that's for sure."

Definitely more here than just professional courtesy.

"Should you have the chance," Hall continued, "tell her I know she's doing stuff she shouldn't. It won't make a damned bit of difference, but I have to weigh in on it or my conscience will bug me. She's on very thin ice with her boss."

"Consider it done."

"To save me digging into our own report, what's your cell number?" he asked. Sam shared it, and then he was the proud owner of not only Hall's number, but also Susan's contact info.

As Sam headed to his own car, he digested everything Hall had told him. Their murder suspect had searched Myers's place and hadn't found what he was looking for, even left behind drugs that he easily could have sold on the street. That told Sam he wasn't after money. He'd also left behind Treina's smashed phone near the crime scene, so what he wanted wasn't on there, either. Where would the killer head next?

The victim's home.

Sam dialed Susan's number, suddenly uneasy.

"Driscoll."

"It's Marsh. Where are you right now?"

"How did you get my number?"

"Where are you? Humor me, please."

"Outside Treina's place. Her sister gave me a key. I was going to check it out and—"

"Not alone," he said, unlocking his car. "Wait for me."

"What? Look, I told you—"

"Susan, don't go in there on your own," he insisted. "Please promise you'll wait for me to get there."

"What's this all about?" she demanded.

Sam pulled out onto the street, even though he had no idea where he was headed. "The cab driver's roommate was found dead in their apartment this morning. The vic had been tortured and the place tossed. My guess is that the killer was looking for something, and since he didn't find it, he could be headed for Treina's apartment next. Or he's already there."

"Probably come and gone by now. You forget, I'm a fully trained federal agent, Marsh. I can handle this on my own."

He heard a car door slam through the phone and sweat broke out on his forehead. "Susan, *please* wait for me." He hated that his voice quavered, but he couldn't prevent it.

Something in his tone must have made the difference. "Okay, I'll wait for you. But once we're done here, you're out of this, you understand?"

Sam sighed so deeply, he almost didn't hear her giving him the address. After he ended the call, his hands still shook while he tapped it into the GPS. The thought of Susan going into that apartment alone brought back too many memories of the night he'd failed his partner.

They'd gone to interview a potential suspect. Always eager, Keith hadn't bothered to wait for Sam to finish his phone conversation with an informant before he knocked on the apartment door. It had proved a fatal error.

Sam had barely reached the landing when an apartment

door opened and a gun appeared. He could still hear the shots as they echoed in the confined space. Feel the solid thud of his gravely wounded partner hitting the floor. Even as Sam fired at the shooter, bullets struck him in the chest. As his lungs had slowly collapsed in that shit hole of an apartment building, he'd pleaded with God not to let his partner die. His prayers had gone unheard.

A horn honk jolted him out of the past and told him the traffic light had changed. As he drove north to Treina's apartment complex, he prayed that Susan hadn't just told him what he wanted to hear.

Treina's Apartment
2:15 p.m.

To Susan's astonishment, Sam Marsh had returned to his usual Zen-like calm by the time he'd arrived at the apartment. Seeing him now, it was hard to believe she'd heard his undisguised fear over the phone. It had stopped her in her tracks, even as she'd been headed toward the entrance to the apartment building. She suspected something in his past had triggered that visceral response.

Need to do a background check on this guy.

When Sam reached her side, he said, "Thank you for waiting."

She expected an explanation, but it didn't come. "Victim was tortured, huh?"

He nodded. "I'm sorry I got so uptight."

"No apology needed. It's the smart thing to do. Thank you for reminding me. Sometimes I get a bit over eager."

No reply.

"Care to tell me why you were like that?"

"No, I don't."

Moving on. "How did you get my phone number?"

"I plead the Fifth on that."

As they climbed the stairs to Treina's apartment—she lived on the second floor—the calm Marsh gradually gave way to an increasingly tense one. When they reached the landing, Susan knew the sweat beads on his forehead weren't just because of the warm weather.

"You okay?" she asked, genuinely concerned.

"Yeah, just not used to the heat."

Which sounded like BS to her.

"You licensed to carry?"

He returned a curt nod. "Full sweep?" he asked.

"Works for me."

Susan waited as her companion removed his gun from his shoulder holster. Carefully unlocking the door, she pushed it open with a foot. Pulling her own weapon, there was an awkward moment as they decided who was going in high, who low. She and Britelli did this instinctively, so this was like working with a brand-new partner.

"Oh, hell," Susan muttered.

They were too late. Their "visitor" hadn't been shy, either. The living room looked like the aftermath of a three-day fraternity party: sofa cushions cut open, stuffing strewn across the floor, pictures off the walls, books off their shelves. Travel posters of Jamaica, Sierra Leone, London, and San Francisco littered the floor. He'd even ripped open the back of the television and done the same with the audio speakers. A dripping sound came from the kitchen, probably the freezer defrosting.

Silently, they worked through the house, room by room. Once they were sure there wasn't a nasty surprise lurking in a closet or behind a door, they stared at the mess.

"No sign of forced entry," Sam said, holstering his weapon. "Must have used her keys."

"He might have left a few prints. Of course, that's only good if he's in the system."

"I'm betting he is. He pulled that trigger way too easily."

It wasn't just the front of the apartment that had been searched. Treina's clothes had been torn out of the drawers, the drawers themselves upended. The closet was empty, hangers scattered on the floor, brightly colored dresses and slacks everywhere. Every shoebox had been dumped out and her jewelry was spread all over the floor. The bed had been torn apart, the lamps overturned.

"Thank God Treina can't see this," she said, shuddering. The sense of personal violation made her skin crawl. From the jut of Sam's jaw, he was pissed. She'd get to that stage soon enough. "What the hell was he looking for?"

"Whatever it is, he's killed at two people for it."

Drifting into the hallway, Susan returned to the room spread in drop cloths. A stepladder sat in the corner. Four short paint stripes had been added to one wall, no doubt to vet the colors.

"Nursery?" Sam asked quietly from the door.

The softness of his voice held a kind of awe. She studied the paint colors, blues and a light beige. "She's carrying a boy, so I'd say yes."

"He has a really strong mother. He'll be in good hands."

She looked back over her shoulder at her companion. "Yeah, he will be. Hopefully this is the worst thing either of them will have to face in this life."

Marsh nodded. "Any more word on the father?"

"None. The family has no idea who he is. Treina was going to introduce her fiancé at her sister's birthday party this coming weekend. But currently, he's still a no-show."

"Please tell me this invisible fiancé didn't get cold feet and order a hit on her."

She grimaced at the thought. "Wouldn't be the first time. But why kill Myers's roommate and dig through his place? If Treina's man had been looking to cover up evidence of his affair, this should have been the only place he searched."

"You're right. This isn't making any sense to me."

"It will. Give it time," she replied. "Stuff like this is why I love my job; it's one giant-assed puzzle, and I have to solve it."

He huffed in agreement. "Talked to Detective Hall today."

Is that how you got my number? "Please tell me you didn't

mention my name."

"I didn't have to. Hall figured it out all on his own."

"Dammit, now Pat's going to be on my ass."

"Pat?" he asked. "Is there something going on between you two?"

"Not now. We dated a few years back. Our careers got in the way."

"As often happens," Sam murmured. "I like him. He isn't an asshole. Some of us are."

"Only homicide guys. FBI agents are never that way."

He snorted. "Yeah, remind me to tell you about the one I met in Seattle. Now there was an asshole with a capitol 'A.' "

As they returned to the kitchen she called in the burglary. In the meantime, Sam closed the refrigerator door with an oven mitt to avoid leaving fingerprints. It wasn't an easy task as the dishwasher had been emptied and broken plates and glasses littered the floor.

Once the call was done, she asked, "So what did Pat want?"

"Said if I was to see you, to remind you that he knows what you're up to."

"Fine. He doesn't sign my paycheck."

"Neither does your mother," he said, frowning now. "You have any way of getting someone to keep an eye on Treina's family?"

"You think this asshole will go after them?" Susan asked.

"Unless our killer found what he wanted here, he's not done. Best to be cautious until he's in lockup, or the morgue."

She thought on that for a time, then nodded. "I'll see to it."

"Officially or unofficially?"

"Whatever it takes."

Chapter Five

Hotel Rosemont
10:40 p.m.

Once the cops had cut them loose, Sam retreated to his hotel room. Of course, as he was about to exit Susan's car, she issued another warning that he was to go play tourist. He blew her a kiss and left her frowning.

Though he knew he needed to do some background research on the victim, her employer, and the cabbie, he gave up and crashed into his bed. The only reason he woke up before the next morning was the evening housekeeper tapping on his door to check if he needed his bed turned down. He politely let her know there was no need and accepted a handful of mints and another bottle of water to mollify her.

After supper he set up his computer on the desk and began his research in an unexpected way: He logged on and read Veritas's final report on the Quinton Ellers mission in South Georgia. Susan's part in it had been impressive. Outstanding, even. Still, he wasn't getting the full picture here. He sent a quick text to Brannon Hardegree, asking him if they could talk. Maybe Brannon could fill in the missing pieces.

As Sam sifted through the available information on the law firm and the various partners and employees, every now and then he glanced at the phone, wondering how Susan was doing. Hoping she might call him, and knowing that wasn't going to happen. His reaction to her was unusual, and he couldn't quite parse out what it meant. He'd admit that some of it was because she was a striking woman, and he certainly wouldn't mind taking their "relationship" in a more sexual direction.

Nevertheless, it was more than that. Despite her prickly exterior, he found Susan intriguing. She had a ready wit, a sharp mind, and eyes that revealed her inner emotions like a mirror. So much so, he'd read that she really hadn't wanted to leave him behind tonight, even as she was telling him to go away. To put it simply, she was conflicted, just like he was.

The thought of her running this investigation on her own made Sam increasingly nervous. Not because she wasn't a pro, but because their murderer had proved to be a cold-blooded son of a bitch. Sam didn't want the bastard anywhere near her.

He glanced at the clock on his phone. Nearly twenty-four hours earlier, he'd witnessed a murder. Somehow, his quiet, stress-free vacation had turned into a nightmare. He took another long drink of water, then went back to his work. If he found the proper bait, Special Agent Driscoll would come to realize that working as a team was their best bet to close this case.

When his phone rang, the display told him it wasn't his favorite FBI agent. He tamped down his disappointment.

"Hey, Brannon, how's it going?"

"Good. How about you?"

Sam rose from the desk, easing the cramp in his back. "Good and bad. You got a few minutes? I'm in Atlanta and I need to know more about Agent Susan Driscoll."

"Is she in trouble?" his friend asked. "Please tell me she didn't get fired."

Brannon's loyalty vibrated down the line. To his surprise, Sam felt the same when it came to Susan. "No, not yet. But if I don't play this whole situation right, she might be."

"Tell me what you need to know. Cait and I owe that woman big time," Brannon replied. "Susan's one of the reasons I'm not sitting in a jail cell. Or that Atlanta's not still counting their dead."

"Okay, here's the problem," he said, then laid out the case from the moment Treina had been shot.

Susan's Apartment
11:24 p.m.

Susan had skipped lunch and eaten leftover lasagna for dinner. Her mother had given her eight squares of it, all frozen, concerned that she was losing weight. Her mom was right. The scale had begun to trend downward ever since the swamp case. A combination of stress, lack of sleep, and the occasional nightmare was taking its toll.

To move this investigation along, while hamstrung because she didn't dare use FBI assets, Susan resorted to her contacts, the ones she trusted not to rat her out. Her request: Tell me what you know about Warburg, Mossman and Day. All off the record, of course.

After a few phone calls, she'd come to understand the dynamics of the firm. Warburg played the genial old Southern gentleman, Mossman was the pit bull, and Day was pretty much known as a nice guy. And all of her contacts agreed that if you were a rich slime ball, WMD was the firm you wanted in your corner.

If I could only talk to them in person. She could read their body language, get a sense of the place and the players. But that move was off the table—one little glitch and they'd call Rhodes to complain. She'd taken a big enough risk letting Marsh know she was with the Bureau.

Now as she sat on her sofa, surfing on her computer, Marsh's odd reaction at Treina's apartment popped into her mind. On impulse she typed his name into her browser, as well as "homicide detective."

The first search result was from the Chicago Tribune, dated about a year and a half earlier. She clicked on the link and stared at the picture above the article: Two paramedics hauling a man out of a building on a stretcher. His shirt was open, his chest a mess of blood, his face covered by an oxygen mask.

She read the caption and whispered, "No."

This was Sam, who had taken multiple bullet wounds to the chest. Skimming the article, she found out that he and his partner had been ambushed. The partner had died on the scene, as had the shooter. Detective Samuel Marsh had barely survived.

That's why you knew how to treat a sucking chest wound.

And it was one of the reasons Treina's shooting was so very personal to him. It also explained why he'd freaked out about Susan going into the apartment on her own, why he'd looked spooked on the stairs. She wasn't the only one with hellish memories.

As if she'd conjured him up, a text appeared on her phone. THIS FOODIE WENT BACK FOR MORE CARNE ASADA TONOC. STILL JUST AS GOOD. SAD YOU MISSED IT.

She snorted. I HAD LASAGNA. HOW'RE THOSE MUSEUMS GOING?

DID YOU KNOW THAT OUR CABBIE WAS ROBBED 2 OTHER TIMES IN THE LAST YR? BOTH CASES HAD THE COPS SCRATCHING THEIR HEADS.

"No!" she said. YOU ARE NOT ON THE THIS CASE!

SO I'VE BEEN TOLD. I KNOW WHERE TREINA WAS PICKED UP THAT NIGHT. DO YOU? :-)

"You little jerk!" Why was he doing this? She gave up and dialed his number.

"Well, hello there. I was just thinking of you," Sam said, as if he hadn't been bombarding her with text messages. "Wish you'd called earlier."

"To tell you to back the hell off . . . *again*?"

He chuckled. "You wouldn't do that, I'm too valuable. But now it's time for bed because tomorrow's going to be a *very* busy day. Goodnight, Susan. Sleep well."

Then he hung up on her.

Her mouth fell open. Mr. Prim and Proper Chicago had just yanked her chain, hard. Before she could stop it, a laugh began, and it quickly filled the room.

"God, you're a piece of work," she said, smiling.

Meehan's Public House (Downtown)
Wednesday, May 13th
2:50 p.m.

Sam had kept up the pressure throughout the morning. It'd been a steady trickle of texts, all related to the case, all of which he knew were driving Susan crazy. He'd refused to meet with her, claiming he was too busy. That also was getting under her skin, as her texts grew increasingly testy.

He'd based his strategy on his conversations with Brannon and his girlfriend, Caitlyn Landry. Cait, as she insisted on being called, had spent time with Susan in the swamp, and she claimed the woman he was seeing in Atlanta wasn't the one she recalled. This Susan was too tightly wrapped.

"Put her off balance. Make her realize that working with you is better than the other option," Cait had said. "She can't resist a challenge. It's not in her nature." Sam had suspected that the same held true for Brannon's new girlfriend. Wimps didn't join the Marine Corps.

So, after finishing off his pan-seared snapper, he sent Susan his final piece of bait. If this didn't work, nothing would.

YOU VISITED THE LAW FIRM YET?

His phone rang within a minute, and that made him smile. She *had* been watching for his texts, not blowing him off.

"No, I haven't visited them," she snarled. Light music played in the background, which led him to believe she was in a coffee shop somewhere.

"What? I'm surprised you haven't leaped right on that," he goaded.

"You know why I can't do that."

"Yes, I do. Gee, wouldn't it be great if you had someone who could? A professional who knows not to push the wrong buttons. In particular, the big red button that leads to your boss."

"Damn you," she muttered. On purpose, he'd hit her right

where it hurt. She didn't dare go near the law firm, or someone might drop a dime on SAC Rhodes.

"You still there?" Marsh asked brightly, knowing she would be strangling him right now if that were possible.

"You play hardball, buddy," she said.

"Only when it matters. You know you need my help. Please just accept it."

A prolonged sigh came down the phone. "Did Pat give you my phone number? No pleading the Fifth this time, Marsh. Just answer the question."

"Yes, he did, but why does that matter?"

"Because that means he trusts you." A brief pause, then a another tortured sigh came down the phone. "Okay, you got a deal. And don't think I like this one damned bit."

It was time to give her ego some cover. "I know. If your situation were different, we wouldn't be having this conversation. You would have handled it just fine. But because it is touchy, we have a better chance of finding our killer if we work together."

"Then let's make that happen, Marsh. I'll be at your hotel in thirty minutes. Be ready." This time, she hung up on him.

Sam grinned. *Challenge accepted.*

Hotel Rosemont
3:15 p.m.

The whirlwind that was Susan Driscoll arrived at the hotel sooner than Sam had planned. He waved her into his room, shirtless. The last time he'd been that way, there'd been only a small lamp on. Now, the scars on his chest were clearly visible.

"Have a seat. I'm changing into a suit. Figured it'd go down better at a highbrow law firm."

Susan settled on the armchair near the bed, watching him too closely. He looked down at his scars, then back up. This was the elephant in the room, and it was time to confront it.

"You do a background check on me?"

"Yes. I'm sorry about your partner."

He nodded, because there wasn't much else he could do. That loss was still too raw.

Sam chose his white dress shirt from the closet, buttoned it up, and tucked it in. Usually he'd pair his black suit with a red tie, but not today. He chose a gray one instead. Somber and serious, that worked best with lawyers.

It was then he realized that something had changed with his visitor. Susan's hair was down, out of its bun, and she wore peach slacks, a white silk top, and a darker peach jacket. A slim gold chain rested around her neck, matching the tiny earrings. Her shoes were white flats. It was as if she'd dressed for a date, not an investigation. He decided to let her know his thoughts on that change.

"You look really nice," he said. "I like that color on you."

"Thank you," she said, eyes warming now as the hint of smile touched the corners of her lips. "It feels weird not to be wearing black or navy."

"If I were director of the FBI, I'd mandate that those colors be banned. At least for the women. Guys in peach could get a bit weird."

She laughed and those caramel eyes seemed to shine now. For a second, he caught a glimpse of the woman Cait had spoken of, the one with a zest for life.

Susan abruptly sobered. "Since this isn't a Veritas case, are you going to get into any trouble talking to the suits?"

"Nope. Veritas is good with whatever I do down here. The legals can rant and rave all they want and Crispin Wilder will just ignore them."

She cocked a head. "Is it true he used to be an arms dealer?"

"Yup. One of the biggies."

"Hmm. He sure saved our asses in the swamp."

"He's known for that kind of thing."

When he turned back toward Susan, she gave him a thumbs-up. "Very GQ, Marsh. That suit looks great on you.

The tie's a bit dull. I'd go for red."

He laughed. "Right with you on that." Her praise made him feel good. "You want to take my car or yours?"

"Mine, and I'll drive. That way you won't get lost."

"Even better."

As Susan worked the car through the late afternoon traffic, she chewed on her bottom lip. It wasn't that she didn't trust Sam, but turning him loose on his own proved difficult. She liked to be in on the action, and the thought of waiting in the car like a flunky made her twitchy.

"You and Detective Hall still close?" he asked.

It was a curious question, but she decided it wouldn't hurt to answer it. "We're friends, but not the kind that come with benefits. I don't like complications."

"Okay," he said, as if filing that information away lest he should ever need it.

"What about you? You dating someone?"

"No. The last few months, the job has been really busy."

"What is it you do for Veritas?"

"Initially, my job was to verify the background research that others had compiled. Sometimes a case is presented to us that isn't entirely on the level. People looking to get even with their enemies, that sort of thing. So I double-check everything. Once that's done, the boss gives his final 'yes' or 'no' on the mission."

"Sounds like a lot of responsibility. You read a situation or an informant wrong and things could go really bad."

He looked over at her now. "Exactly. There are times I worry that I've missed something vital, something that might get our people killed. I've also served as backup on a couple of missions. That doesn't happen very often, but it's nice to get out of the office from time to time."

"So, on a scale of one to ten, how much do you love your job?" she asked.

"Nine. The only reason it's not a ten is that the hours can get long sometimes. But once the report is in, I can take a few days off and recharge, so that's good."

She knew he'd ask the question.

"What about you and that ten scale?"

"Right now, it's about a six-point-five. It was closer to an eight-point-five when my old boss was alive."

"So why not find a new place and start over? There has to be a bureau chief who is more like him than your current head."

Susan didn't reply, because he was uncomfortably close to something she'd been thinking about ever since she'd returned from South Georgia. She was thirty-three and she'd lived in Atlanta her whole life. Sure, she'd traveled, both for business and pleasure, but she felt increasingly tied down. It didn't help that all of her siblings were married now. The subtle pressure to do the same was starting to grate, one family dinner at a time.

"You know, I'm pretty sure Chicago has an FBI office," her passenger said, his tone suspiciously innocent. "You'd know someone there, right off."

"Nice try, but you have real winter up there." She pulled into a parking lot and turned off the car. Looking over at him now, she took in the complete package. In jeans or in a suit, this guy was handsome. Confidence radiated off him. Right now, she could use some of that.

Susan made a shooing motion. "Go make me proud, Marsh."

"And if I don't?" he asked.

"Then it's a long walk back to your hotel."

With a bark of laughter, he exited the car, then straightened his suit coat. Susan watched him walk toward the entrance in the rearview mirror, shoulders back, every inch of him indicating he knew exactly what he was doing.

At least one of us does.

Chapter Six

Warburg, Mossman and Day, P.C.
4:00 p.m.

As their website had indicated, Warburg, Mossman and Day's offices covered six floors of a high-rise commercial structure in Midtown. A good-sized firm, one moving ever higher in the legal pecking order.

The firm's founder, Charles Warburg, was in his seventies, clearly edging toward retirement since he spent at least one day a week on the links. Edward Mossman was gearing up to take his place, while Robinson Day was their newest partner. On the website, at least, clients raved about their services.

Adopting his detective demeanor, Sam pushed through the heavy glass door that led into the building's lobby. The security guard eyed him, then seeing the suit, no doubt decided he wasn't a threat. Which was a mistake; often white color criminals were more dangerous than street thugs.

After signing in and having the guard check his driver's license, he was waved toward the elevators. Shiny marble flooring accompanied him on that journey, along with enough mirrors to make Snow White's evil stepmom envious. He resisted the urge to leave a few fingerprints behind. As he rose to the tenth floor, there were stops along the way as not-so-eager worker bees got on and off the elevator. Two women, in particular, were chatting about Treina.

"I can't believe she got shot," said the first one. She was in her mid-twenties, at most, and had a breathy sort of voice.

"It's getting too dangerous in this city," the other one said. She was older, but both were in conservative dresses and heels.

"I heard that Mr. Day is out of town. I wonder if he knows what happened yet," the younger woman added.

"Who knows? You'll never find out from Ott, that's for sure."

They got off at the seventh floor, still chattering about Treina. Sam smiled to himself; it was apparent the two were not fond of Gail Ott, Mossman's executive secretary. The not-so-good news was that Day was out of town.

Now it was up to Sam to charm more information out of the denizens of the tenth floor. The entry to that exalted location featured more marble, expensive leather chairs, and a secretary whose tailored suit probably cost more than his monthly mortgage payment.

She eyed him with polite indifference. "How may I help you?"

"My name is Samuel Marsh," he said, sliding a business card across the counter. "I'm a private detective and I'd like to speak to someone who works with Treina Wilson please."

As the woman stared at him for a moment and he made sure to deliver one of his most pleasant smiles, signaling that he understood how this all worked and was willing to play along. The receptionist reached for the phone and made a call, and when it ended, she gestured toward one of the leather seats. "Someone will be out to help you shortly. Would you like something to drink?"

Sam did, preferably something with caffeine, but he shook his head. He'd expected foot dragging, general BS, and being shown to the door. The fact that they were actually going to have someone talk with him was both encouraging, and suspicious.

He picked up *The Economist* from the small table next to the chair. The article on artificial intelligence caught his notice, and he skimmed it as he waited. Curiously, it proved to be quite informative.

"Mr. Marsh?" a voice called out.

He reluctantly set the magazine aside and rose. "Yes?"

Gail Ott approached him now. She looked much like her photo on the website, only a few years older. From what he'd gleaned online, she was forty-six years old, divorced, no children, and had been with WMD for over twenty years, beginning as a secretary.

Her black hair was cut short, her dark eyes were piercing, her cheekbones a little too sharp. She had tried to soften those with her makeup, but it didn't quite work. Her muted teal suit was certainly not off the rack. Everything you'd expect in an executive secretary in a top-dollar legal firm.

"I'm Gail Ott, Mr. Mossman's executive secretary," she said. "If you'd come this way, perhaps I can answer any questions you may have."

"Thank you, I appreciate your assistance."

Sam was led into the inner sanctum, down a hall, then into a room marked "Private." Another pair of leather chairs awaited him, and he chose the closest. Ms. Ott sat across from him after she'd closed the door.

The room appeared to be a private lounge of some sort, though very well appointed. A box of cigars sat on a credenza, bottles of expensive scotch and bourbon on the bar. The wall opposite them was a solid bank of glass with a postcard-worthy view of Atlanta. Apparently, this was where the high rollers met with their attorneys. No plebeian office setting for their legal needs.

To Sam's surprise, his phone pinged a distinctive triple chime. The special app on his cellphone had just registered an active audio bug nearby. Did Ott know about that? He bet she did.

He made sure to keep his face neutral, and to weigh his words even more carefully. "I appreciate your time, Ms. Ott," he said. "I know you're a busy person."

"I'm not sure why you're here. Isn't Ms. Wilson's robbery being investigated by the police?"

"It is. However, I was present when she was injured, and her family has requested that I conduct an investigation as well.

They have some concerns."

"I see. I don't know how I can help you."

Ms. Ott's tone of voice was guarded, and not overly sympathetic. If someone in Veritas's home office had been wounded like this, the others would be upset and very angry. That wasn't what he was getting here.

"What are Treina's duties for the firm?"

"She is Mr. Day's paralegal."

"He handles civil cases, right?" A quick nod returned. "Does she have any involvement with criminal cases?"

"None."

The answer came a bit too fast for Sam, which made him wonder if this was true. "Have there been any cases recently that might have impacted her private life?"

"I don't follow."

"Let's say that one of your clients wasn't pleased by something this firm did on his or her behalf. If that was the case, they might have sought a means to get even."

Ms. Ott huffed, clearly irritated at his suggestion. "Nonsense. Our clients are all upstanding businessmen and women."

Bull. "Regis Neager certainly wasn't," he said, using some of the information he'd dredged up the night before. "He was trafficking kids to pedophiles. Some of those children were as young as three."

The woman's expression remained neutral, despite the sickening topic. It must have taken her years to acquire such a poker face. "Mr. Neager's case never came to trial."

"How fortunate for him." Sam shifted back to the topic at hand. "Would you have any idea why Ms. Wilson might have been at Atlantic Station last night?"

The woman hesitated. "Of course not. I don't keep track of our employees after hours."

"All right. We're trying to locate her fiancé. Do you happen to know who he is, and how we can do that?"

She shook her head. "Ms. Wilson was very private about her personal life, and we encourage that at this firm."

Again, her reaction flew in the face of how office culture really worked. When guys became engaged, their fellow males heckled them good-naturedly and demanded an invite to the bachelor party. For women, there was jubilant celebration and lots of hugs. It was that human touch, which Sam was beginning to think was lacking at WMD. Or at least with this woman.

"Has Ms. Wilson been overly nervous or upset recently?" he asked.

"Of course she has. She's pregnant. Why wouldn't she be?"

He'd give her that one. "Is Mr. Day in the office? I'd like to talk to him, if possible." Not all elevator gossip was on the money.

His question made Ms. Ott sit up straighter. "No, he's not. Besides, I don't see the point. He wasn't in town at the time of the incident. Why would you need to speak to him?"

"Because bosses often know things about their employees that others do not." Crispin Wilder certainly did.

"Not in this situation. Mr. Day will be out of the office for the remainder of the week. He's working on a very difficult case."

"When did he leave?"

She frowned now. "Monday."

The day Treina was shot. "Is he aware that his paralegal is in the ICU?"

"Yes. I spoke with him yesterday. He was quite concerned."

Her tone was off, higher pitched now. That could indicate stress, and since she knew him to be a PI, that was understandable. *Or maybe you're lying.* It was hard to tell which.

"May I leave a message with his executive secretary to have him call me?"

"Heidi is on vacation. You can leave it with me."

This woman had a PhD in stonewalling.

"That's okay, I'll check in with him once he's back in town. Well, I think that's about all I need to ask. I do appreciate your time."

Mossman's secretary gave a curt nod and rose. As they stepped outside the room, a woman called out to his escort. Ott stepped aside to talk to her.

Sam eyed the rest of the office, taking note of those employees who were paying close attention to his presence. One young man, in particular, took considerable interest in him. He gave Sam the once-over, smiled, then returned to whatever he was doing.

What was that all about?

Ott cleared her throat and he turned toward her. "Mr. Mossman would like to have a few words with you. If you'll follow me."

Sam trailed along like a dutiful puppy, making note of everything he saw, filing it away for later reference. As was often the case, more money did not always equate to good taste. Edward Mossman's office was an excellent example. Though not overly large, it featured an exuberance of cherry wood. Desk, shelves, you name it. The solid wood paneling, massive windows overlooking the city, and a desk that had to weigh a ton, were clearly meant to impress.

In Sam's case, it all failed. He'd been in Crispin Wilder's office, which was understated, though well appointed. Nothing this ostentatious, because Wilder knew true power wasn't found in possessions.

Mossman rose, adopted a fake smile, and walked around the desk to greet Sam. He was about six feet, trim, with whiskey-colored hair that probably required more styling products than was wise. The lawyer's handshake was brief and as fake as his smile.

"I hope Gail has been able to answer all your questions," he said. "This is such a tragedy."

"She has been very helpful. I was hoping to speak with Mr. Day, but apparently he's out of the office."

Mossman's eyes flicked to his secretary and then back again. "Yes. He has an important civil case in Colorado."

"I see."

"Such a shock. I understand it's still touch and go."

"I was hoping to visit her," Ms. Ott said. "But the hospital said only family is allowed at present."

That warm-and-fuzzy concern was at odds with her attitude only a few minutes before. Was it mere theater for her boss?

"I'm sure you'll be able to visit Ms. Wilson soon," Mossman said, his eyes going to her again. It was as if there was some invisible conversation Sam wasn't privy to.

"This case in Colorado. Is it fairly straightforward?" he asked.

"I would assume so. Rob doesn't say much about his clients unless their activities are more criminal than civil."

"I see." Sam easily read the vibes in the room. He'd been allowed to kiss the ring of one of the bigwigs; now it was time for him to leave and never darken their halls again. "I should be going. Thank you for your time."

"Very glad to meet you. Let us know what we can do to assist you. Whatever it takes to help Ms. Wilson's family feel better at this most difficult time," Mossman replied.

God, what a tool.

As he turned away, Sam noticed a picture on the desk, a family photo with the wife and a couple of kids. That meant Mossman wasn't Treina's fiancé, not unless he wanted a very expensive divorce.

Once Sam was on the elevator headed down to the lobby, a ping came from his phone, a single one this time. That was probably the FBI agent in the parking lot. Frankly, he'd figured the text would have come a lot earlier than it did. As he exited the building, he removed the phone from his pocket and read her message.

FYI – HOSTAGE RESCUES ARE MY SPECIALTY. YELL IF YOU NEED HELP.

Sam broke out in laughter. This lady had game, and a really wry sense of humor. No wonder a crazed anarchist hadn't gotten the better of her. As he approached her car at the far end of the parking lot, the door locks clicked open. Once he was inside, Susan gave him a single raised eyebrow.

"Well?"

"No rescue needed."

"I got that. You're in the car; that's a big hint. So what happened?"

"Let's just say it wasn't a wasted trip. Get me coffee and I'll talk. Can we go somewhere near Atlantic Station?"

"Sure. Why there?"

"Sorry, I thought I told you. The dispatcher said that's where Treina was picked up. Maybe we can figure out what she was doing there and that'll give us something."

"Okay, but Atlantic Station is not just one place. It's a planned community with businesses, apartments, and a mall. She might have been there shopping, stocking up on pantyhose for all we know."

"Without her own car?" he asked.

"Good point. Maybe the reason we haven't found it is because it's out there." Then she shuddered. "God, I hope not. That place is huge."

As she headed west, Sam related his conversations with both Ott and Mossman. Then he told her about the audio bug in the private meeting room.

"Okay," she said, frowning. "That's legal here in Georgia. We're a one-party consent state, so I'll assume Ott knew of the recording, and that'd make it kosher. It still feels weird to me. How did you know there was a bug?"

"I have a phone app that notifies me if there's an audio or video signal within thirty feet or so. It's saved my butt a few times."

"Sweeeeet. Your employer's doing?"

"Yup. One of the perks of working for them; they got all the cool tech. The app looks like a game, so if someone glances at the phone, they have no idea what it really does."

"Did Mossman or Ott have any clue who her fiancé is?"

"If they did, they decided not to share," he replied. "I find it interesting that the day someone tries to kill her, both her boss *and* his executive secretary are out of town. Might be coincidence, or not. Robinson Day is in Colorado, by the way."

"Huh. Maybe I can track him down," Susan replied.

A quick glance told Sam they were on 14ᵗʰ Street, headed west. As they crossed over the interstate, it was jammed with cars. He remembered the photo on Mossman's desk. "So do you think this fiancé is on the level?"

"Why wouldn't he be?"

"All this secrecy. Maybe he's buying time with the ring until he can lose Wife Number One. Or it's all a scam to keep Treina on the hook until he dumps her."

"Whoa, that's a buttload of skepticism there. That happen to someone you know?"

"Scenario Number Two did. I had a cousin who got screwed over by a guy who strung her along, then ditched her. Claimed the baby wasn't his until the paternity tests proved otherwise. Getting child support out of him has been hell. I'd love to see him at the bottom of Lake Michigan, encased in a concrete suit."

She gaped at him. "You didn't just tell a federal agent that you'd like to cap some dude, did you?"

"No, I just told a federal agent that I'd love it if someone *else* did. There's a difference."

"Any likelihood of that happening?"

"Yes," he said, grinning now. "The fool didn't realize that my cousin's stepfather is with the mob. I think the only reason the loser's still alive is that Angela doesn't want him dead. One of these days, that won't be the case and then he's fish food."

Susan laughed. Her whole face changed when she did, her eyes lighting up, her white teeth a nice contrast with her tanned and lightly freckled skin. "We *so* didn't have this conversation. Especially the fact that you have mob connections."

"I don't, at least not directly. My dad's from Chicago and my mom's from New Jersey. It was inevitable that someone would have a distant relative in one of the crime families."

"Mr. Law and Order has a dark side. I'm impressed."

He grinned. "What about you?"

"Not much. A few moonshiners and someone who was part of the Underground Railroad. Other than that, we're a boring bunch."

"That I doubt."

He found that he loved listening to her talk. Susan's voice had a rich, earthy timbre, with that honey-light hint of Southern drawl. She could read the nutritional information off the labels on canned goods, and he'd savor every word.

Before he could stop himself, he yawned, barely covering his mouth as he did.

"You really must need caffeine."

"Definitely." Yes, he needed the java, but right now, he needed her company more.

Land of a Thousand Hills Coffee Co.
Atlantic Station
5:30 p.m.

Susan's choice of coffee shop was perfect. It had the proper vibe, right down to the "Drink Coffee, Do Good" slogan on some of their cups. On impulse, Sam ordered peach bread pudding, then asked for two spoons. They chose a table near the window and settled in. He pushed one of the spoons over to her and was pleased when she began digging at the pudding. Sharing food seemed almost intimate in some way. Sam knew they should focus on the case, but this just didn't feel like the time.

"Ever been married?" he asked, leaping into the deep end. Her eyes popped up from the dessert.

"No. You?" she replied.

"Nope. Any brothers or sisters?"

"Two sisters and a brother. And what is this? Vet the date or something?"

"Oh, we're on a date?" he said, grinning. "I didn't realize that."

A tiny frown appeared between her brows. She probably thought it made her look serious, but in truth, it was simply endearing. "Why are you being charming?"

"I'm being charming because I'm spending time with an

intelligent woman who also happens to be quite pretty."

He received a series of blinks at that. "You're hitting on me?"

"No, I'm enjoying your company, and the fact that I'm alive, especially since I could have bought a bullet Monday night. In case you haven't noticed, you *are* really smart and pretty. A winning combo for sure."

Susan went quiet after that, as if she wasn't accustomed to being told such things. Or it was her habit to ignore them out of hand.

It wasn't until they were in the car that she said, "Thanks. For the compliments, I mean. I usually let those kinds of comments slide by. I don't like to be distracted."

"And in this case?" he asked, turning toward her.

The tiny brow wrinkle reappeared, Susan's "tell" that she was thinking through the question, rather than annoyed. "Not sure. I'll get back to you on that."

That's a start.

6:15 p.m.

Of course, Susan had been correct—Atlantic Station was a large, multipurpose development that, according to Sam's phone surfing, covered almost one hundred and forty acres.

"So where do we begin? The mall, or at one of the restaurants?" he asked.

"I suspect we can safely rule out the gay strip club west of here."

"Perhaps," Sam replied, though he never excluded anything until forced to do so.

He was known for being painfully systematic, a trait that had driven his fellow cops nuts on occasion. Still, his attention to detail had made for solid convictions when his cases went to court. Even now, he could still annoy his co-workers at Veritas when he insisted something didn't feel right and wanted the hard data to back up a particular claim. They razzed him about his nitpicking, but they understood that his skills might keep those in the field alive.

After Susan parked, they walked through the open-air shopping mall. Initially, she was cruising along at a fairly fast pace, no doubt fueled by the bread pudding's sugar load. Sam made sure to move slower, forcing her to slow down. Hurrying wouldn't get him what he needed. Besides, it seemed she felt the urge to rush through life, as if she'd miss something. Or maybe she was hurrying so something wouldn't catch up with her. He couldn't tell which.

Wandering around seemed to annoy her, and being Susan, she voiced that annoyance. "So what's the plan here, Marsh?"

"For me, just getting a sense of the place."

"Which helps us how?"

He had to remind himself that this case was personal to her, more so than for him. "You don't do something like that?"

Susan thought on that. "Yes, but not like you. From what I can see, it's like you've opened a mental file drawer and you're dumping unnecessary crap into it."

He frowned over at her. "I won't know which details are unnecessary until further down the line. You do the same, you just aren't aware of it. Except you do it a lot faster than I do."

"Ah," she said, but he couldn't tell if that was an "I understand what you're saying" or a "just get on with it, will you?"

As they passed another shop, he backed up to study the dress in the window, then the woman he was with. "You'd look really nice in that."

Her eyes moved to the display, a sleeveless sundress in pale beige and black with bright red splashes. If he guessed right, the hem would reach to just below her knees, allowing her trim legs to show to their best advantage.

"We are not here to shop," she said, frowning.

"Not into multitasking?" he asked, just to needle her. *So damned serious.* What would she be like if she cut loose?

Her eyes went to the dress. "Yes, it's nice, but I don't see the point."

"You're too mono-focused, so you're missing things. Like how pretty this dress would look on you."

"Marsh," she began in a warning tone.

"And how this shop sells clothes in the same vibrant colors and styles our victim had in her closet."

Her mouth dropped open, then closed quickly. "Point taken. How's about we check out that dress?"

He opened the door for her, making sure not to look smug.

The clerk did recognize Treina, said she had shopped here often, but that she hadn't been in the night before. Susan had pointedly *not* tried on the dress displayed in the window, even though she liked it, a lot. Maybe she would after Marsh went back home. If she bought it, she'd think of him every time she wore it. Was that a bad thing?

Over the course of another hour they went into the more promising shops and she showed Treina's pictures to the sales clerks. Some remembered her, some didn't. None had seen her the night before.

They were strolling back to the car—at the speed Sam moved, she couldn't call it anything else—when her phone rang. It was her partner, Joe.

"Hey guy. What's up?"

"Nothing. Just checking in."

"You did that this morning."

"What? Your partner can't do a welfare check but only once a day?"

"You can. But really, what's up?"

"I wanted to know what you're working on, because I know you're not home painting your nails and watching soaps."

"Do people still do that? The soaps, that is?"

"My mother does," Joe said. In the background, she could hear bar noises. He was probably playing pool at his favorite watering hole.

"I'm checking out something for a friend."

The noises in the background dropped considerably, which

meant he'd probably stepped outside. "Is this the kind of thing that's going to get you fired?"

Lying to Joe was not an option. "Probably, if Rhodes finds out."

"Dammit, Susan, you know better—"

She cut him off, then gave him the overview of the case so far.

"Warburg and Scum? Really?" He paused. "What can I do to help?"

She'd known he would say that. A sideways glance showed that Sam was surfing his phone, no doubt listening to her side of the conversation. She'd be doing the same.

"I'm good so far. I've teamed up with the guy who witnessed the shooting. Former homicide detective. Only one problem: He works for Veritas."

"Holy shit. You really do want to lose your job, don't you?"

"No, but I want to find out why someone tried to kill Treina. I swear there's more to all this than just some robbery."

"I agree. Let me do some quiet digging on this end. It'll take me a while. Rhodes has me doing follow-up on the Ellers case. We're trying to hunt down any of his cronies who are still in town. Me? I figure they've gone back under their respective rocks, but she insists there might be a few more waiting for the chance to cause mischief."

"I hate to say it, but she might be right."

"Yeah, that's what I'm worried about. So where are you now?"

"I'm at Atlantic Station with Mr. Marsh."

"Making it a date?" her partner teased.

"That's the second time I've heard that word tonight. And no, it's not. Look, I gotta go."

"Okay. Stay safe. 'Night, Suz."

Only he got away with calling her that. Well, he, her mother and one ex-boyfriend.

"'Night, Britelli."

Sam looked up from his phone.

"That was Joe, aka Guiseppe Britelli. He's my partner and a

second-generation Italian. He's a kick. You two should meet."

"I'd like that. We can trade Agent Driscoll tales. I bet he has a few."

"Yes, and I have a few on him, too."

"Did I hear the word 'date'?" he said, which told her he'd overheard some of her conversation. From his grin, she could tell he was messing with her. "Sure you don't want to buy that dress now?" he added, his eyes twinkling.

"No, but go ahead and buy it for yourself, if you think they have your size."

His carefree laughter accompanied them down the street, and it triggered hers. Sam made her feel special, like she wasn't just spinning her life's wheels. She liked those traits in a guy, especially one who didn't treat her like she was nothing more than a Barbie doll with an FBI accessory badge. Somehow spending time with this man seemed to polish off some of the tarnish on her soul. She couldn't figure out how, but he just did.

Pity the PI was heading back north soon. Maybe she *should* buy the dress, if for nothing more than to remember how much she'd enjoyed his company.

Chapter Seven

Atlantic Station
8:00 p.m.

Something had been nagging at Sam all evening, something to do with timing. He put his question to his companion just as they reached her car, the heat of the day gradually cooling around them.

"Help me here: The shops close at nine. Treina was shot at nine forty-five, give or take a couple minutes. How long would it take a taxi to go from here to my hotel at that time of night?"

"During the week?" she said. "Not that long. Probably ten to fifteen minutes."

"So what was she doing between the time the shops closed and she was picked up?"

Susan scrunched up her face at that. "Assuming she was shopping, and that's a huge assumption, maybe she wandered around? Or waited until a cab rolled by to head back home?"

"Maybe," he said, frowning as he closed his door. "We're assuming she was here in the mall, but what if she was at a restaurant? Maybe meeting her fiancé?"

"I like how you think, Marsh. Let's see what we can find out," she said.

Thirty minutes later, they both knew this wasn't working. Sam had popped into each restaurant, shown the hostess a picture of Treina on his cell phone, and then walked back to the car with his dejected "I got nothing" expression.

After the last restaurant, Sam leaned his head back against

the headrest, then bounced his skull off it a couple times like an annoyed child. "Zip, *nada*, not happening," he said.

"Keep going, or bag it?" she asked.

"Call me stubborn, but let's keep going a little bit longer, okay? How's about we cruise out a little further?" He was back to staring at his phone now, typing something on the screen.

"Seeking divine help?" she said.

"Yes, from the Great Lord Google. We've tried the stores and the restaurants. How about a club? There's a place called Secrets and Lies. It's about a mile from here."

"I've heard of it. Supposed to be *the place* if you're into kink."

"Really?" His eyes narrowed. "What sort of kink?"

"A little raunch for everyone, and they card you at the door, which should tell you something. Apparently, there's a whole separate part of the club with a special membership, if you're into BDSM and some of the more 'exotic' stuff."

"Sin in the Bible Belt," he said as she turned the corner. "I'm shocked, I tell you. We don't have that kind of thing in Chicago. Nope, not at all."

"Riiight."

It was easy to find the club, not so easy to locate a parking place. Susan drove around until one became open and claimed it without hesitation.

"This is a long shot, you know," she said as they exited the vehicle.

Right now, he was willing to try anything.

She noticed his somber mood. "Hey, you okay?" she asked, touching his arm.

"Just remembering Monday night," he said, his eyes distant now. "If I'd gotten to her sooner, I might have been able to—"

"Do what? You weren't armed, were you?"

"No," he admitted.

"So what were you going to do, stun the killer with stats about the White Sox?"

Sam looked down at the pavement. "No, I would have

probably gotten shot, dead even."

"Exactly. I know it's hard to let go of the guilt. Hell, I never do. But in this case you worked with what you had."

His eyes rose to meet hers. "Thank you. I need to hear that more often." He studied her for a moment. "Maybe you're doing the same guilt thing about the swamp mission? Am I right?"

Susan nodded. "I keep asking myself how I could have prevented those deaths."

"And?"

"I couldn't have," she replied. "I don't know about you, but that makes me feel damned angry."

He looked toward the building now. "Yeah, I know how that goes."

To her surprise, as they headed for the front door, he caught hold of her hand, squeezing it once. "Glad you're still around. Atlanta wouldn't have been the same without you."

She squeezed his hand in return. "Same to you, Marsh."

Secrets & Lies
9:30 p.m.

Susan barely hid a yawn behind her hand, and then Sam had to fight the impulse to join her. They'd been waiting for almost forty-five minutes, during which he'd amused himself by crowd watching, listening in on conversations. It was a cop thing, and now a PI thing. Mostly, he watched the type of people who were eager to get inside the club, and the bouncers who manned the door. Or "personed the door" in this case, as one of them was female.

Susan was watching them as well. "Is it just me, or do the bouncers look like they're with the Secret Service?"

That would be an easy assumption what with their black suits, white shirts, ties, and high-tech earbuds. Security cameras were in place as well, four of them that Sam could see.

"Why didn't you ask the security folks about Treina when you were up there?" she asked.

"They seemed too serious to pony up any details and would probably just kick us to the curb. Figured we'd have a better chance inside, with one of the servers." If he was lucky, she'd just go with that explanation. But of course, she didn't.

"And . . . ?" Susan nudged.

Sam sighed. "All right, you got me. I wanted to check out the club."

"I knew it! Which level did you choose?"

"Level One—Voyeurism. The lady said it's nude, exotic dancers with a lot of high-tech special effects."

Susan eyed the building. "Truth is, I'm kind of curious myself. I've been in strip joints and brothels, but a really high-end sex club? No. I'm wondering who their clientele is."

"People with serious disposable income."

She looked over at him. "What was the cover charge?"

"Thirty." He paused. "*Each.*"

"What?" she spouted. "This better be pretty damned special."

"Agreed. Would this even be the kind of place Treina would frequent?"

Susan thought on that. "My guess is this isn't, at least not with what I know of her. But we're here, so we might as well check it out. I'll pay you back for the cover."

Sam didn't reply since he didn't intend on collecting that debt.

"My college roommate was an exotic dancer who worked at a fancy club," Susan continued. "She brought home money like a Wall Street banker. She'd count out the bills on the kitchen table, putting them in tall stacks. She earned enough to pay for her tuition and her books, and kept physically fit in the bargain."

"Those are all good things."

"Most people think it's an easy job. I did, at least until I tried working a pole during amateur night and damned near killed myself."

He grinned. "I bet you were great. I would have tossed a couple bucks your way."

"Not even close to great, but it was for my sister's hen party so it was worth the bruises."

"You stay in touch with your friend now?"

"I do. Liz works at a big-name law firm in Portland. Specializes in domestic abuse and divorce cases."

"Good for her. No problem with her employers over her former job?"

"No. She told them right up front how she put herself through school, then showed them her high-octane grade point average and her pristine FBI background check. Told them if they couldn't deal with all that, she'd go somewhere else. The head of the firm was so damned impressed, he hired her on the spot."

At that, the pager he'd been given—it was in the shape of a pair of lips—began to buzz and flash so they presented themselves to the woman at the podium.

"Mr. Marsh?" the woman said.

"That's me," he replied.

She checked out Susan, then went back to her list. "Level One Voyeur?"

"Yes, please."

"First time?"

"Yes, at this club, at least," he replied. He could feel Susan's eyes on him at this point.

"Great! We hope Secrets and Lies lives up to your every desire."

So far, it'd only lived up to waiting in line, but who knew what might happen once they were inside. According to those idling along with them, this place had a reputation for being "wicked." Hopefully, he'd find out if "Atlanta wicked" was the same as back home.

Their escort into the club was a buxom blonde, sheathed in a black lace bustier, little tap pants, and black fishnets. Her heels allowed her to look down on him like an Amazon.

"Follow me, please," she said, and set off. Sam forced his

eyes off her rounded butt and made them focus further north. That proved difficult.

The doors automatically opened, like at a big-box store, but instead of the bargain of the week on an endcap, they were greeted by a young woman in a dress that they'd probably stolen from an upscale porn video.

"Welcome!" she said, smiling broadly. "I'm Sunny."

Sam's attention was still on the dress. It consisted of a silvery and gold mishmash of strips that wound around her body, no doubt held in place by strategically placed double-stick fabric tape. The bust line ended just north of her nipples, the bottom strip barely below her black lamé thong.

"God help her if she sneezes," Susan muttered.

Sam stifled a snort. They were led down what looked suspiciously like the yellow brick road from *The Wizard of Oz*. He half expected to see a flying monkey or two. Gradually, the yellow bricks morphed into green, then blue.

Their escort paused in a central foyer from which five doors led off, like spokes on a wheel. Above each door was a sign indicating what type of activity could be found behind it, and there was a black-suited bouncer in front of each one, the beefy kind that meant business.

Sam's eyes scanned the signs, and he was pleased to see that no new vices had been invented since he'd last been in an adult club for a murder investigation. Each generation always thought themselves more wicked than the previous, but the truth was that humans had been dreaming up naughty activities since they'd first crawled out of the caves. Probably even before that.

Sunny veered off at this point, leading them through an arched doorway marked Port Voyeur. Sam wasn't sure what he'd expected, but this wasn't it. The individual tables were made of some kind of brushed metal, rising up from the floor, then crowned by a clear Lucite top. Instead of chairs, there were benches, also metal. Once he and Susan were seated, they were handed off to a server who said her name was Linnea.

"This looks cool," Susan said, nodding in approval.

"The floor show begins in twenty minutes," the server said, smiling. "While you're waiting, here's the menu."

She pressed a button on the tabletop, a section of it opened, and a tablet ascended, just like you'd expect in a Star Trek movie. Sam mentally gave the place points for style.

"This is your communicator," she said, indicating toward the tablet. "Go ahead and tap the upper right-hand corner.

Sam did so with his index finger, and the screen lit up with the S&L logo, a brassy sort of in-your-face design that someone had been paid a lot of money to create.

"Just access the menu, fill in your names, pick what you'd like to eat, and then swipe your credit card. We're fully automated. I'll bring you some complimentary Perrier while you're doing that."

Then she was gone.

"Not what I thought it'd be. It's like spaceport chic," Susan said, looking around.

When she began to shimmy out of her jacket, he helped her and then placed it on the bench. Looking around, Sam realized he was seriously overdressed. He removed his tie and stuck it in his suit coat pocket, but didn't take off the coat because of his shoulder holster.

"That's better," she said. "Now you fit in."

Sam stared at the tablet as it blinked ENTER NAME(S) PLEASE.

After he'd entered his first name, a glitzy menu appeared. After some pondering, he chose a beer from their extensive list and a plate of potato skins because he wasn't that hungry. Susan selected a glass of wine. None of this was fancy—however, the prices were, which maybe was part of the appeal.

Once he'd finished placing his order, it prompted Sam to pay with his credit or debit card. Pulling out his wallet, he swiped his card along the side of the tablet, then signed with his fingertip.

ALL SET, SAMUEL appeared on the screen.

"Thank you," Susan said. "I didn't expect you to pay for my food."

"Not a problem. So what do you think? Is this a hotbed of illicit activity or just a jazzed-up bar with overpriced drinks?"

She leaned forward, resting her elbows on the table, her chin in her hands. "Not sure." Then she grinned. "Look! A hen party. That means there must be male dancers in the show or they wouldn't be here. This could be a lot of fun."

Sam's gaze followed hers to the next table over where four young women were just being seated. One, a blonde, wore a tiara and across her ample chest was a white and gold sash that said "Bride to Be." The ladies sounded as if they already had a few drinks under their garter belts, their voices loud and high pitched.

"I love this place," one of the women said, a dark-haired beauty with a tan that wasn't quite natural. "It's just so cool. Let's order our drinks, then do the quiz. They've always got great questions, and they change all the time."

"Quiz?" Susan said, then looked down at the tablet.

Sure enough, there was a blinking icon. Sam touched it and a screen popped up. The questions started with the "Since This Is Your First Time Here, Let's Get to Know You" section, which included the opportunity to win free drinks.

Susan leaned against him to see the screen better. He could feel her warmth, smell her light perfume. Sam made a mental note not to rush through the questions—not if she remained where she was.

"Why would a place give away free booze?" she asked.

"PR, I guess."

At that moment, Linnea delivered their drinks and Perrier, urged them to take the quiz, then retreated. From the sounds of the ladies next door, they were gearing up for a long night. Smiling to himself, Sam took a sip of his beer, savoring the bright hop notes.

He offered Susan the tablet in case she wanted to answer the questions first, but she shook her head. "Go for it."

"Why did I know you'd say that?"

He worked through them, one by one: Was he from Georgia, and if not, where did he live? Was he single or married? Straight, gay, bisexual? When it was completed, it awarded fifty points toward another drink, which made him wonder just how many points you had to have to earn one.

"And this is fun, how?" he asked.

Susan bumped him. "Lord, you're worse than me. Chill out, will you?"

The role reversal caught him off guard. Usually, she was no-nonsense. That told him she'd needed an evening out, even if it was case oriented.

"There has to be some point to all this," he said. "A company does not invest in software like this just to keep their diners happy while someone is making the fries."

"Airlines have those trivia quizzes."

"They do that so you don't rebel because you're jammed in their planes with less room than a sardine in a can. Distraction is a great anger-management tool."

Another quiz popped up. This one was far less generic.

His eyebrows rose as he skimmed the questions.

"What are they asking now?" she asked.

"Ah, on average, how many times a week do you have sex with another human being?" he blurted, blinking in surprise.

Susan's laughter tickled his ear. "This place *is* called 'Secrets and Lies,' remember?"

"Yeah, but this is getting personal."

"Ah, come on. Go for it," she said.

"Only if you do the same."

Now it was her turn to be flustered. "What? No way. Not happening."

"Not so cool when it's *your* libido on parade, is it?" he chided.

She eyed him, and from the look in her eyes, she'd just accepted his dare. "What are the choices?"

He looked back at the screen. "One to two per week, three through six, and 'I should be in therapy for sex addiction.'"

"Seriously?" she said, leaning closer, her breast brushing up against his arm again. If he were a gentleman, he'd move that arm, but that wasn't happening.

"They also have a 'zero times per week' option. There's a sad face after that one."

"As there should be." Susan sighed. "Me? On average?" Her cheeks colored, and for a moment he thought she was going to chicken out. "Zero. At least over the last year."

A beautiful woman like her? It was his turn to be surprised. "I am sincerely sorry to hear that."

"You're not the only one, Marsh. What about you?"

"Probably two to three times per week, more if I'm really into the lady. It all depends on my schedule. If I'm doing background for a case, then it's no nookie." He sighed. "It's been that way for the last few months." He turned back to the screen and clicked "1 – 2," figuring that was a safe average.

"Hey, at least you're better off than I am. What's the next question?"

"Favorite positions?"

"Okay!" she said, beaming. "This should be a blast."

Even before he could reply to that, there was a commotion from the next table. The hen party had ordered a big pitcher of something purple and frothy, and was going through it at a rapid pace.

"It wants to know if I've ever slept with a friend's boyfriend or husband," the bride said, giggling. "I don't know if I should answer that one."

"But if you do, you get points toward a free meal," one of her friends replied.

"Okay." All her girlfriends leaned closer now, some more steadily than others. "I slept with my fiancé's boss. Do you think that counts?"

Sam whistled under his breath. "I hope the poor guy did a prenup."

"No kidding," Susan replied.

He nearly cried out in joy when the food arrived so he could ignore the quiz. Though, to be honest, he'd love to know his companion's favorite position, and why.

"Hopefully, Ms. Bride's hubby-to-be isn't the jealous kind," Susan said, "or he might not be too pleased when he finds out his boss has grand slammed his future wife."

"Grand slammed? Is that some sort of Southern term?"

She winked at him. "If you're a good boy, I'll tell you some others."

The club grew a lot warmer, and he reached for his beer to cool down.

"So what *is* your favorite position?" Susan nudged.

He nearly choked on his brew.

She asked.

He made sure to catch her eyes. "Mine? Any position that has my lover begging to come . . . for the *third* time in a row," he said.

Susan's breathing picked up, her brown eyes widening. "Damn, Marsh, that was one helluva answer."

"Sam. If we're talking sexual gymnastics, we're definitely on a first-name basis."

"I agree. Sam."

As he returned to his beer, his own heart rate faster than it had been a few minutes before, Susan's eyes never wavered from him. No doubt, she was working out just exactly how those three orgasms might happen, because he certainly was.

The conversation cooled down a bit after that. They talked about the food—the potato skins were good, with just the right amount of cilantro and asiago cheese.

Linnea floated up to check on them. "Everything fine?"

"It's all good," Susan replied. "Your quizzes don't pull any punches."

"Wait until you get into some of the later ones. They're really out there," the server replied. "Not that you guys need it, but you can find yourself a date here. The quizzes match you up with people who are in the club at the same time you are. It's very high tech."

"I must be old fashioned, then," Sam replied, wiping off his fingers on a napkin and gazing over at Susan now. "I like to do my date-finding the hard way."

"Well, if you change your mind, you'll find all sorts of interesting people at Secrets and Lies."

"That I wouldn't doubt," Susan replied.

"You need a refill on your drinks?" They both shook their heads.

"However, if you could do us a favor," Sam began, quickly pulling up Treina's picture on his phone. "Did you see this woman in here the night before last?"

Linnea sat on the bench next to him. "Yeah, I did. She was talking to some stuffy lady."

"What did this stuffy lady look like?"

The server scrunched up her face in thought, chewing on her lip now. "Dressed in a suit, an expensive one. Black hair, serious resting bitch face. A dom, for sure, if you know what I mean."

Sam did, and that opened up another whole direction into this case. "If I show you a few pictures, could you tell me if one of them is her?"

"Maybe," the server said. She looked over at the neighboring table, then nodded when the bride indicated they wanted another pitcher of whatever they were drinking. "I can't stay long, though."

"No problem. I'll make this quick." Sam pulled up the employee photos from the law firm, then handed the phone to the server. Linnea scrolled down with a finger adorned with a long silver fingernail. She pointed. "This is the one."

Gail Ott.

"Well, I'll be damned," Susan murmured.

"I've seen this guy in here, too," Linnea added, scrolling back up. The face she gestured to was that of Edward Mossman.

"Well, well, well," Susan said, looking over Sam's shoulder. "Seems lawyers got kink, too."

"Did you get any idea of what the two women were talking about?" Sam asked.

"No. The younger one looked angry. There was no love lost between them, that's for sure." The server hesitated for a moment. "Sorry I can't tell you more. I had a table with a bunch of geeks from Georgia State. They wanted to play grab-ass, and that's so not in my job description."

Before Sam could follow up, the lights dimmed and the curtains pulled back to reveal a stage at the far end of the room. Behind it was a huge video screen. Music soared and then laser lights began to dance around.

"Ladies and gentlemen! Welcome to Port Voyeur!" a voice called out.

Women began to appear on the stage, one by one. Each was wearing an outfit that might have been perfect on a space station, provided it was into G-strings, thongs, and bare breasts.

"Okay," Sam said, winking at Susan. "This works."

"And here I thought you were a Boy Scout."

"Are you kidding me?"

"Oh look! *That's* better," Susan said as four men appeared on the stage now. They were buff, tanned, and all wearing leather thongs and black studded collars. The bride-to-be and her cohort screamed in excitement.

"A little something for everyone," Sam said, savoring the gleam in Susan's eyes.

"Not a *little* something. Check out that guy on the right. He's built."

Sam did, then sighed. He'd never be that guy, muscle-wise or otherwise. Just genetics. His eyes strayed back to one of the dancers, a pretty brown-haired girl. As he watched her work her routine around one of the male dancers, he couldn't help but clap and shout his encouragement.

"They're good," he said.

"And suitably raunchy," Susan replied, her eyes riveted on the show.

As promised, the production was high tech, acrobatic, and full of lots of highly toned and nearly nude bodies. Over time, all ten of the dancers wandered through the crowd. Sam noted that the women refused anything close to a lap dance. When the brown-haired one visited their table, he struggled to keep his eyes above her ample breasts. And failed.

He shifted on the bench seat, his pants suddenly too tight. The dancer winked at him, planted a kiss on his cheek, then moved on to the next table. The bride stood and danced with her, executing an impressive drunk shimmy.

Susan's turn came when the guy she'd been eyeing came by. As soon as he offered his hand, she shouted "Yes!" and shot up to join him, bumping hips. Her hair lit up like fire in the spotlights, her breasts straining against her silk top, as pure sexual energy poured off her.

Damn, woman.

The dance ended too quickly, at least for Sam. Susan plopped down on the bench seat with a husky laugh. "That's the closest I've been to an orgasm in ages."

Then she grabbed him and planted a kiss on his lips. He returned it just as eagerly. Over her shoulder, he saw the male dancer shoot him a thumbs-up.

When the show ended, to raucous applause and catcalls, a "tip jar" popped up on the tablet in front of them, one for the entire cast.

"What do you think?" he asked.

"Kick in a hundred and fifty and I'll split it. Those are tomorrow's lawyers," Susan said.

He laughed. "You got it." Even before he finished the transaction, her share of the tip, plus her cover charge, came his way across the table. He pocketed the cash, knowing not to argue. As the lights came back up and Sam found himself reluctant to leave. "You kissed me," he said.

"Yes, I did," she said simply. And that seemed to be that.

Once he'd helped her put on her jacket, they headed for the entrance.

"That was really fun," he said.

"Yeah. I liked it a lot. Why the hell haven't I ever come to this place before?"

"Too much work?" he said.

"Sadly, yes. Too much work, not enough life."

"Who knew that alien princesses had a thing for space pirates?"

"Very well-equipped space pirates," Susan said, waggling her eyebrows. "That guy had to be enhanced, right?"

"God, I hope so," Sam said. "If not, I should just join a monastery now."

She squeezed his arm. "I doubt that. But then, I haven't seen the evidence first hand."

If Susan had had more than one glass of wine, he'd have figured it was the alcohol talking, but that wasn't the case. Not knowing how far to push it, he held this silence as they exited the club. Once they were outside, he could almost see her retreating into her shell.

"Think the valet might know something?" she asked.

With an inner sigh, he acknowledged that their moment had passed. "Let's find out."

As they approached the stand, a young Black man in a valet's uniform offered them a quick smile. Probably a student at one of the local colleges, working his way through school.

"Can I get your car for you?" he asked.

"No, but maybe you can help us." Sam showed him Treina's photo. "Did you see this lady the night before last?"

The man studied the photo and nodded. "She had me park her car. It's still here. It wouldn't start."

Susan traded looks with her partner. "Any idea why?"

"Sorry, I don't know."

"Did you see her get into a cab?"

"No. I offered to call for one, but the lady she was with insisted she'd find her a way home."

"Was this the lady?" Sam asked, showing Ott's picture.

"That's her. Real tightly wound, you know? The younger woman didn't seem to like the idea, but the older one kept pushing her, so they left together."

"Any way we can see the car?" Susan asked.

The valet winced. "No, I'm sorry. And I'm not saying that to shake you down. I need this job, and that's a sure way to get me fired."

"I understand."

There was no choice now, not if they wanted the information. "Maybe this will make it easier for you." Susan extracted her badge and ID from her purse and let the valet see them. Out of the corner of her eye, she caught Sam's worried look.

The valet's eyes widened as he realized exactly who he was talking to. "Well, ma'am, it looks like I can help you. The valet lot is behind the club. You know the make and model?"

"I do. Any chance we can get the key."

"Ah, no. I'm thinking that's a step too far. Sorry."

"Got it. I'll let the local cops know where to collect the car. Thanks, we appreciate it."

"Why are you asking?" the young man said. "Did that lady make it home okay?"

"No, she didn't," Sam replied. "She was shot after she left here. She's going to make it, but we want to know why she got hurt."

The young man sighed. "Helluva world we live in."

"That's for damned sure," Susan muttered.

Chapter Eight

Atlantic Station
11:30 p.m.

The club's valet parking was crammed with high-end cars, mostly BMWs, a Lexus here and there, and a few sports cars.

"Some of these are damned nice," Sam said. "Glad I don't have their car payment."

"There's a red Honda," Susan called out, pointing. As they moved closer, she added, "Tag number matches."

"Nothing looks out of place," he said as he walked to the front of the vehicle, careful not to touch it. "The hood is up just a bit, like someone didn't get it closed properly."

"Which you would expect, if the car had some problem with it."

"Or if someone tampered with it." Sam went down on his hands and knees, peering under the vehicle. "I'm not seeing anything obvious like big pools of fluid or anything, but then, my knowledge of cars is purely basic." He rose and dusted off his slacks. "Someone might have cut a wire somewhere, or messed with the battery."

Susan carefully leaned against the BMW behind her, making sure not to trigger the vehicle's alarm. "So the valet tells her the car won't start. If it were me, I'd call roadside assistance or my family. If she didn't have AAA, why didn't she call her sister?"

"Didn't want them to know she was at a strip club?" Sam suggested.

"Maybe. Why get in a cab with Ott?"

"You're assuming she did. Wouldn't it have seemed strange to her that Ott hung around while the valet was getting her car?"

"I wait around until I know my girlfriends are headed home safe. Ott might have framed the situation that way." She typed out a text message. "I'm letting Pat know we found the vic's car."

Sam rubbed his chin. "If Ott stayed with her, ensured she got into *that* particular cab, the robbery was preplanned. Myers just needed to drive her to a set location, where our shooter was waiting."

Susan's phone rang. "Hey, Pat."

"So where is the damned thing?" he asked.

"In valet parking at Secrets and Lies."

There was a long silence. "You there now?"

"Yes. The floor show was educational," she said, just to needle him.

"I bet. Marsh with you?"

"Sure is. He didn't even blush once. Who knew?"

Sam shook his head in dismay.

"We found witnesses that place Edward Mossman's executive secretary at the club with the victim," Susan added. "According to the valet, once it was known Treina's car wouldn't start, Gail Ott insisted on finding her a cab."

Another long silence on the other end of the phone. "Mossman? That son of a bitch. You think this is all tied up with him?"

"Don't know. Sam visited the law firm today and got major runaround. When he talked to Ott, she failed to mention that she'd been with Treina a short time before the shooting."

"Huh. Did he talk to the vic's boss?"

"No, Mr. Day is out of town, as is his executive secretary."

"We got that stall, too. Damned convenient, if you ask me," Pat replied. "We'll make another run at the law firm, see if we can rattle some cages."

"Talk to the Secrets and Lies people. Mossman is enough of

a regular that a server knew him."

"That doesn't surprise me. Probably loves getting flogged after a tough day of fucking over cops." Pat hesitated and she knew that meant he was going to ask something she wouldn't like. "You and the PI a thing now?"

"Is that professional curiosity, or something else?" she asked.

The detective sighed down the phone. "Sorry, the question was off limits. I'll head over your way once I get a warrant. Can you stay with the car until then, or do I need to send over a couple uniforms?"

"We'll stay put for now. If it gets too late, I'll call you and you can send someone over. The valet has the key."

When she ended the call, she found Sam watching her closely.

"He want to know if we're grand slamming?" he asked.

She grinned. "Something like that. Why?"

"When he talked about you, Hall showed deep regret. I know if it were me in his shoes, I'd feel the same."

Susan opened her mouth, but nothing came out. How did you follow up on something like that? Instead, she retreated to her safe corner. "Pat will be here soon to eyeball the car."

"Do you always dodge personal things by hiding behind your work?"

"Don't you?"

He gave a low whistle. "Okay, I'll give you that one. May I suggest you file a preliminary report with your boss so she knows what's going on?"

"Yeah, that's *just* what I want to do. That way Rhodes can preemptively suspend my ass rather than waiting until down the line."

"I don't know your relationship with her, and it doesn't sound the least bit good, but everything is telling me you need to make the first move, that it might save you a butt-ton of grief. It's only a matter of time before the law firm figures out you're connected to this case, and they'll rat you out for sure. It sounds like their style."

Susan frowned at him a few moments longer, then groaned. "You really think that's a good idea?"

"Whoever set up this hit has some clout, and that power is going to be dropping on both of us like a load of bricks. They can't hurt me—Veritas won't allow it. You're the vulnerable one right now."

He was right. Rhodes would most likely go ballistic if she found out about Susan's "off the books" work through another source. Or maybe not. It was hard to know with her. "Okay, but when I get fired and I'm homeless, it's on your head."

"You get canned, come see me in Chicago. I'll give you the gold-plated tour, take you to my favorite pizza joint, and give you a place to stay while you start over."

She stared at him. "You serious?"

"Absolutely," he said, quieter now. "I've grown fond of you, Suz. I would hate to have you rattling a tin cup on a street corner somewhere."

He must have overheard Joe calling her that on the phone. "Susan. I don't like Suz or Susie."

"Okay. For the record, I detest Sammy, so please don't go there."

She smiled. "I won't. I promise."

Susan certainly wasn't going to be begging on the street if Rhodes canned her. One upside of not having a personal life was that she didn't spend that much money, other than for necessities. Her nest egg was large enough to buy her sufficient time to find another job.

Still, Sam's offer, a genuine one it appeared, had touched her heart. Without thinking, she leaned closer and brushed a kiss on his cheek. "Thanks for offering me crash space in Chicago."

He touched her hair fondly, and for a second she thought of kissing him again. To her disappointment, he stepped back.

"Don't want to be in a clinch when Detective Hall arrives, now do we? I have no desire to spend the night in a cell with a bunch of gangbangers."

"Pat's not that vindictive."

He shook his head, as if she was naïve. "Oh, honey, all guys are sore losers. Some of us hide it better than others."

Thursday, May 14ᵗʰ
1:00 a.m.

Susan stifled a yawn. In retrospect, she should have had Pat send a couple of beat cops to babysit the car.

Live and learn.

She sighed in relief when he finally arrived.

"Marsh," the detective said, then ignored him as he turned toward Susan. "You did good work today."

That aggravated her. "*We* did good work. Mr. Chicago was in on this, too. He's not just eye candy." A barely contained snort came from Sam.

"I'll take your word on that," Pat replied. "Sorry it took so long to get the warrant."

He took off his suitcoat and handed it to Susan. Then he pulled on a set of nitrile gloves, retrieved a plastic evidence bag from his pocket, shook out the key he'd claimed from the valet and unlocked the door. Once inside the car he tried to start it. That effort failed.

"Okay, then," he muttered.

The detective opened the hood and peered down into the interior. Bending, he rummaged around for a few minutes, then retreated. "Someone removed one of the fuses."

"So it was premeditated," she said.

"Looks like it."

"Can you pop open the trunk for me?"

"Sure."

A quick check proved there was nothing out of the ordinary there. In particular, no shopping bags, so most likely Treina had come to Atlantic Station solely to meet Ott.

"Detective?" Sam called out. He stood near a vintage

Mercury Sable in pristine condition. "Would it be a fuse like this one?" he asked, pointing.

Pat trudged over, stared at an object lying on the ground, then nodded. "That's it. You have good eyes. Suz, there's an evidence bag in my suit coat pocket. Can you grab it for me?"

She rolled her eyes at his shortening of her name, then did as he asked. Pat collected the fuse and dropped it in its own bag. Closing the hood, he locked the car and then stripped off the gloves. To complete the process, he leaned against the hood of the Sable and filled out the required information on the outside of both evidence bags.

"At least now we know why Treina Wilson was in that cab," he said. He looked over at Sam. "What can you tell me about this Ms. Ott?"

"You didn't get to talk to her when you were at the firm?"

"No. I got Warburg's secretary, who is probably as old as he is. She gave me a big fat zero. I requested that Ms. Ott call me, but so far I haven't heard from her."

"My take? She's a stone-cold bitch," Sam replied, "and trust me, I don't use the 'B' word that often. If she set up Treina to get hit, she's trying to protect something or someone."

Pat huffed. "Please tell me this all has something to do with the firm. I'd love nothing more than to see those assholes in prison. God, I'd even start attending Mass again just for that."

"Well, you might get your wish. FYI, the club is bristling with security cameras," Susan said. "That should help you out."

"I'll have Randy check them out tomorrow morning, provided he's back at work."

"He sick?"

"Yeah. Remember how I told you my partner is a human garbage can, that he'll eat anything? Well, he tried some Chinese food that had been in his refrigerator for God knows how long. He's really sick this time and is swearing he'll never do it again. I give him a month." Pat gave her companion a quick look, and then his eyes returned to her. "Thanks. This helps us get a little bit farther down the road."

That sounded like a dismissal, so Susan and Sam headed back to her car. A quick look back proved Pat was still watching her, even as he was on the phone to the towing company.

Sam murmured, "Told you."

It took her a moment to realize what he meant. "We parted on good terms."

"But who ended it? You or him?"

"Me. He's a great guy, but the chemistry wasn't right."

"Like I said, he regrets it. Smart man. I've been there too, once upon a time."

Susan would have liked to ask about the one that got away, but she decided it was best left in the past. It took some time to reach the car, and as she drew closer, she clicked her remote. The car honked, the lights came on, and the engine started.

Sam shook his head in dismay. "I've never understood the purpose of that. What's the point? You'll be in the car in what, a minute or so? Why start it from over here?"

Susan hadn't really ever given it much thought. "I think it's cool. Just because you're stuffy and old fashioned doesn't mean other people can't enjoy technology."

Fortunately his phone pinged, drawing his attention to it. "Got an e-mail from Veritas marked 'Urgent.' They don't usually do that unless it's a big deal."

As he read the message, she pulled away from the curb and headed toward downtown.

"You slimy bastard," he growled.

"What's going on?"

He frowned over at her, clutching his phone tighter than usual. "Mossman is what's going on. Because it isn't always wise to tell people I work for Veritas, there's a separate phone number and e-mail that I use if I want to run in stealth mode. That way if someone researches me, they'll find I work for a company called Wayne Enterprises. That's what was on the business card I gave Ott this afternoon."

"Wayne Enterprises? Like in Batman?"

"Yup. The security folks at Veritas have a weird sense of

humor. So tonight, 'Wayne Enterprises' received a phone call demanding to talk to my boss. Alex Parkin—he's a former DEA agent—took the call to screen it. Apparently, Edward Mossman gave him an earful."

"Really? So what did you do? Pillage and burn your way through the law office? Ravage a few secretaries along the way?"

His anger must have slipped down a couple notches since he chuckled. "According to Mossman, I was rude and belligerent, and I made all sorts of unfounded accusations. I must have really rattled them because he said that if I wasn't pulled off this case, he'd be calling the State of Illinois to demand that my PI license is revoked."

She whistled. "They Googled you and found out you used to work homicide. If you'd been an everyday PI, I doubt they would have tipped their hand this way. They're spooked, and that makes me wonder why," she said. "This is actually great news, Sam."

"I know, but it still pisses me off. Of course, Alex played along and sincerely apologized. He told Mossman he'd talk to me about it and have me back off to buy me some time. Alex said I owe him a couple glasses of bourbon for having to deal with the dickwad."

Susan laughed. "So how do we bury the dickwad? Because I want to be in on that, even if Mossman has nothing to do with the shooting."

Curiously, a smile formed on Sam's face. "Thank you for sharing my outrage. As to how we bury him, Mossman made a huge error. Alex let my boss know what's going on. Crispin *hates* bullies, especially rich ones. So instead of pulling my ass back to Illinois like Mossman hoped, he's allocated resources to our investigation. Even now, they're conducting a full background check on the partners and Ott. We should have the results in a few hours."

"Oh, hell, yes!" she said, knowing exactly what that meant.

"Which means there's even more reason for you to file that report with your boss tonight."

"Dammit you're right."

She could just imagine what Rhodes would say if she knew Veritas was directly involved in this case. She looked over at her companion now, seeing his anger had ended, replaced by quiet resolve. No, Sam Marsh was not the kind of guy you wanted as an enemy. He looked pretty harmless, but there was a warrior underneath that suit and tie. One who would happily gut his foes and let them bleed out at his feet. Fortunately, she was on his side, because she'd hate to ever become his enemy.

Once they arrived at the hotel's front door, he unexpectedly leaned over and placed a light kiss on her cheek. "How's about we do breakfast and compare notes?"

"Sure. I'll pick you up and take you to Sweet Melissa's in Decatur. They've got great food."

"Perfect." Sam hesitated as if he had something else to add, then got out of the car. He waved as he walked into the lobby, and for a moment, she wished they didn't have this investigation weighing them down. She would join him in his room, find out if he was as thorough in bed as he was about everything else. No surprise, the vivid images that flooded her mind made her blood heat.

Susan shook her head to clear it. Daydreaming about a handsome guy who was headed home in a couple days wasn't the brightest idea. On the other hand, if they did get hot and heavy, he was headed home in a couple days, so there would be no strings attached. Who knew? Maybe by the time Sam left, he'd know *her* favorite position.

Hotel Rosemont
1:30 a.m.

After stopping at the front desk to retrieve his computer from one of the hotel's safe deposit boxes, he took the stairs to his room, smiling all the way. Mossman had made a mistake, and that meant he had something to hide. Whether that had anything to do with Treina's shooting was unclear, but it was a start. The arrogant fool had no idea who he'd messed with when he'd stepped on Veritas's tail. He was about to learn.

The other reason Sam was smiling was because of Susan. They'd covered a lot of personal distance tonight, almost all of it on her part. Maybe when the case was over, they'd go on a real date. If he could guess her size, he'd even buy her that dress he liked so much.

"Yeah, dinner, dancing, and then making love all night," he murmured to himself. He knew that would be incredible. He'd seen the fire in her eyes at the club, and it told him she'd be amazing in bed.

Humming to himself, Sam slid his key card into the lock. As the door swung open, he reached for the light switch and then stopped. Something felt wrong. It took a second for everything to register, and then he swore. Someone had been in his room, and this person hadn't left a mint on his pillow.

"Oh, hell!" he said.

The mattress had been flipped off the box springs, the sheets, pillows and comforter thrown to the side. Pictures were off the walls. Sam's clothes were strewn all over, his suitcase upended, and the drawers in the bureau emptied. The intruder had even dumped out the ice bucket. The faint smell of urine filled the air. Luckily, he'd trusted his instincts and stored his computer at the front desk.

This vandalism was a logical progression: Treina's place, the cabbie's apartment, now Sam's hotel room. The three people who'd been at the shooting. Where would the guy go next if he didn't find what he wanted?

Susan's apartment.

If she didn't have an alarm system, she could walk in on the killer, unaware of the danger. Sam stepped out into the hallway, let the door close behind him, fumbling with his phone.

"Hey, miss me already?" she said teasingly.

"Are you home yet?"

"No, why?"

He sighed in profound relief. She was safe. That was all that mattered.

Susan's Apartment
3:00 a.m.

Susan had told Sam not to worry, that she had a state-of-the-art alarm system that would send her a warning if someone had breached her apartment. That had only marginally reduced his worry. He'd finally stopped fretting when she'd called back to tell him that her place was untouched and insisted that he should come to her apartment once he was free of the cops. He'd agreed, as the glower he'd received from the hotel's night manager indicated that he was no longer welcome at the Rosemont.

Once he'd dealt with the pissy manager and answered all the cop's questions, he'd had to find his clothes in the mess and repack them. Now, two hours later, Sam texted Susan from outside her door, not wanting to knock and possibly wake up her neighbors. He was exhausted.

When the door opened he could tell she'd showered—her hair was still damp, with a light curl at the ends. She was dressed in a soft pink T-shirt and black yoga pants, her feet bare. Her toes had bright-red nail polish, but she wasn't wearing makeup, which suggested that maybe she wasn't quite feeling the chemistry between them as much as he was. He felt a pang of disappointment, even as his nose caught the faint scent of magnolia.

"Come on in," she said, waving him forward. He rolled his suitcase inside, placed it out of the way, and set his computer bag on top of it.

"He didn't take your laptop?" she asked, surprised.

"Couldn't. It was stored at the front desk."

"Smart move."

He finally had a reason to smile. "I thought so. I appreciate you offering me a place to sleep. I'll go hunting for another hotel room tomorrow. The Rosemont's management is not really happy with me right now."

She huffed as she headed into the kitchen. "Then they better beef up their security. They have video surveillance?"

"Yes. The cops are going to check it out. They also have a sizable amount of DNA now." She turned, catching his annoyed tone. "Our thief pissed on my favorite pair of jeans."

Susan's mouth tipped up in a smile. "I'm sure you'll get them back down the line. After a few washings and—"

Sam shuddered. "The guy also ripped up a few of my shirts. He's losing his cool, and I bet that's because he's getting some serious pressure from whoever is pulling his strings."

"That's all good, then. Well, except for your clothes. Coffee or tea?"

"Tea. You got decaf? I'm not going to be upright too much longer."

"I hear you."

It finally registered that there was music playing in the background. "You like jazz?" he said.

"Absolutely. Ever been to the New Orleans Jazz and Heritage Festival?"

"No, is it good?"

"Very. We'll have to go there sometime." She froze for a second, as if she'd just realized what she'd said, then continued on making tea as if nothing had happened.

Sam hoped she hadn't made the offer just to be nice. It'd be wonderful for them to take a long weekend in the Big Easy. They'd stroll the streets, eat at street-corner cafes, make love all night . . . Of course, another part of his anatomy thought that was a great idea so he pushed aside those erotic images before she noticed.

As they chatted back and forth, comparing artists and songs, Sam checked out her apartment. It certainly wasn't what he'd expected for this no-nonsense sort of lady. Based on her tailored suits, he'd guessed her style to be lean and clean, with no fuss or frills. Instead, her decor was more Old World than modern. An antique clock sat on the mantel of her stone fireplace, the pendulum swinging back and forth to mark the seconds. Next to that was a delicate china shepherdess figurine, crook in hand and a lamb at her feet.

Above that was a painting of the Atlanta skyline, done in pale watercolors. The bamboo floors were covered by throw rugs, and the sofa was a rich emerald green. Not a bit of glass or chrome in sight. He suspected this was the side of Susan Driscoll that few saw.

A cup of chamomile tea in hand now, he headed toward the one wall that held the family portraits. It was easy to follow Susan's progression from a smiling toddler missing a couple teeth through to her high school graduation, then on to college and the FBI Academy. There were bridesmaid photos as well, one with someone who looked to be a close relative. One of the sisters maybe?

As Sam turned to study the remainder of the front room, his eyes paused on the menorah sitting on a bookcase. "You're Jewish?"

"Yup, a genuine 'Red Sea pedestrian.'"

He smiled. "Monty Python lover, as well?"

Her eyes sparked. "You too?"

"Definitely. I'm a Unitarian Universalist, so we have no theological issues to hammer out."

"You do your thing, I do mine," she said, nodding. "We're probably both wrong, but what the hell."

Sam chuckled. "Exactly." His phone rang and he didn't even have to look at the display to know who it was. He'd been figuring he'd get this call since he'd reported the break-in at his hotel.

"Marsh."

"Sam, it's Crispin. Thought I should talk with you about what's going on down there."

"It's getting interesting, that's for sure. Serves me right for taking a vacation."

"Probably why I haven't had one in years. First thing, we will be sending you background on Warburg, Mossman, and his secretary within the next few minutes. Also, on Mr. Day and Ms. Wilson. Will that help?"

That was fast. "Definitely."

"We're also compiling a list of cases that have been handled by the firm since Mossman bought in. He has an interesting background: He used to be a vice cop in LA."

"Huh. That means he knows how to find the right people to do his dirty work."

"That's what I thought. Does Ms. Driscoll's boss know she's involved in this case?"

"No." He looked over at Susan at this point. "I suggested she rectify that problem ASAP."

"Is she with you right now?"

"Yes. I'm staying at her apartment tonight since the hotel thinks I'm a hazard."

"I'd like to speak to her, if possible."

Sam covered the phone and relayed the request.

"Sure. I'd be happy to talk to him."

He handed over the phone and addressed his tea, wondering what his boss was up to.

"Ms. Driscoll. Good to finally speak to you."

"Same here. I owe you and Veritas so much for what you did for us in the swamp."

"As we owe you. However, now I need to ask a favor."

His accent was hard to pin down. She thought she heard Britain in there somewhere, but it was so muted she might be wrong.

"Name it." It didn't matter if it was legal or not, she owed this man her life, and the lives of countless others.

"Please do whatever you can to keep Sam safe. I know he'll deny he's in any danger, but the more I'm hearing, the people you are investigating have connections in certain criminal circles. You being with the FBI will grant you some protection, but he's running solo at the moment." Wilder paused. "Sam has probably already told you that I'm allocating resources on this end to help with this investigation, but I currently can't shake anyone loose to watch his back."

She heard the regret and knew how that felt. "I'll take care of it. I promise."

"Now comes the part you will not want to hear: You can do that more effectively if your boss knows what's going on, because I suspect that Mossman's next move will be to notify SAC Rhodes of your involvement."

Susan sighed. "Sam's already put the screws to me, so I'll be sending in my report tonight. That way she'll know what's going on."

"Excellent. In the meantime, please let us know what information you might need. We have many sources that we can tap a lot quicker than you trying to get a warrant for the same information."

"Which means a lot of this is under the table," she said.

"That would be *broadly* true," Crispin replied, though she heard the smile in his voice. "Will that present a problem for you?"

"Me? Not in the least. It'll only matter if we go to court. If it involves the law firm, they know about a zillion ways to get the case tossed from the get-go."

"Understood. I'd appreciate anything you can do on that end. Just keep Sam safe and I'll consider us even. He's one of a kind."

She looked back at her companion, who was currently scrutinizing her bookshelf. "Yes, he is."

The call ended and she placed the phone on the kitchen counter. "You have a good boss."

"One of the best. What did he want to talk to you about?"

"Keeping you alive."

He stared at her for a moment, a copy of President Jimmy Carter's *A Call to Action* in his hand. "I wondered if that's what he was up to. I always trust Crispin's instincts because they're excellent." He held up the book. "What did you think of this?"

It was quite the non sequitur, like he was uncomfortable that someone would go to so much effort on his behalf.

"I found it thought provoking," she replied. "If you'd like

to borrow it, go ahead. You can mail it back down to me when you're done."

He seemed to appreciate that gesture. "I will. Or you can pick it up when you visit."

"You mean when I'm job hunting?"

"Job hunting, sightseeing, or otherwise, you're always welcome at my home," he said.

It was clear he meant every word. "I'll keep that in mind. Consider it payback for appearing on my doorstep in the wee hours."

"Hah! You did it first, remember?"

He had her there. It was time to get back on the case.

"As far as I can see, the most pressing things we need to know are who is Treina's fiancé, and where is he?"

"I agree. I'm really interested in why Day and his secretary are out of the office over the exact time period that Treina was shot. Supposedly, he's in Colorado. If that's not a lie, a partner for a firm like that is not going to fly commercial."

"I have a contact at the FAA. If he took a charter, I might be able to score us a flight plan."

"Good." He set the book on the counter next to his phone. "But first, you need to write a report, don't you?"

She rolled her eyes. "You can be a pain, you know that?"

"You'll thank me down the line."

Chapter Nine

Susan's Apartment
4:00 a.m.

It might have been any other evening at home: Susan curled up on the sofa, a cup of tea nearby as she proofread the report for her boss, triple thinking every word. Next to her, nursing his own cup, was Sam, surfing through reports that had poured into his inbox. He seemed at home with her, totally at ease. That she felt the same way with him was remarkable. Trusting someone wasn't easy when you were a fed—you knew too much about human nature.

Over the years, she'd learned that some men had a "wearing in" period, much like a new pair of shoes. They pinched and chafed until you found a way to cope. Some never adjusted and you moved on. To her surprise, she and Sam "rubbed along" very well, like they'd always been together. She wasn't quite sure what to make of that, and from his reactions, it appeared he didn't either.

Finally, after a brief silent prayer, she hit the send button on her e-mail, suspecting she'd probably just trashed her career. Out of courtesy, she e-mailed a copy to Britelli, because her partner needed to know what she'd done. She could just imagine his comments as he read through it.

Sam stirred, gesturing toward his laptop. "This is Mossman's background dossier. I'll give you the highlights: Only child, graduated at the top of his class in high school. Was a vice cop for a few years, had more than his share of complaints from the public. An Internal Affairs investigation came back inconclusive, but some believed he'd been on the take. Earned his law degree, worked in LA for a couple years, married, had two kids, then bought into the partnership here."

"Financials?"

Sam raised an eyebrow. "That would require us hacking his bank accounts. I don't think it's wise for me to admit that's an option in front of a federal agent."

"Oh, hell, just do it. I won't tell anyone. If we need them, we'll get a warrant for them."

The eyebrow descended now. "On paper, Mossman's worth about three million. House is paid for, worth about one and a half mil. Our accounting people suspect he has an offshore account or two. They're working to find those now."

He initiated the shutdown procedure for his computer, shaking his head in resignation. "I'm fragged. Do you mind if I take a shower and then go to bed?"

"You're a guest. Do whatever you'd like. My house, your house."

"Thanks."

Sam pulled his shaving kit out of the side pocket of his suitcase, along with a pair of yoga pants. He knew this shower was more to put space between him and Susan than for cleanliness. Dammit, he was a professional and he should have been able to keep his mind on task. Not with her around.

As he'd been telling her about Mossman's finances, he'd watched how she moved, how her trim legs curled underneath her on the sofa. How her long fingers curved around her teacup. Then there was the scent of her. Magnolia. God, he'd never see a magnolia tree the same way for the rest of his life. Each inhalation only made him want her more. He'd tried every conceivable way of telling his body to chill the hell out. And failed. So a cold shower was his last resort.

After he'd dried off and dressed in his yoga pants, he stepped outside the bathroom barefoot, his other clothes in a tidy pile in his hands. He frowned—the living room was dark.

"All clean?" she asked, leaning in her bedroom doorway. Susan wore a pale-blue silk robe that ended mid-thigh, her brown hair hanging over her shoulders, the robe peeking open to give him a view of her nightgown and her peaked nipples.

He swallowed heavily at the sight, which had just reversed all the effects of the chilly shower. "Yes, thanks." He'd figured he'd be sleeping on the couch. Did this mean . . .

In answer to his unspoken question, Susan crooked a finger, beckoning. "The bed's this way."

Sam took a deep breath, then followed her. The bed was turned down, one of the boudoir lamps lit. He set his clothes on a nearby chair, then turned to her.

"Just so I'm not reading things wrong—am I here to get some sleep, or to show you my favorite position?"

She looked up into his eyes, then ran her tongue over her bottom lip. "What do you think, Sam?"

Reaching out, he touched her cheek. "I think you are a very dangerous woman, Susan Driscoll. You've gotten inside my head, and I don't know how to handle that."

"Then you're thinking too hard," she replied. "Just let this be what it is."

She stepped closer, then lightly touched her lips to the corner of his mouth. He accepted the invitation, kissing her deeply as his hands tangled in her hair, the feeling of silk between his fingertips. Susan molded herself to him now, her own hands roaming down his back and inside his pants. Her fingers gripped his butt and pulled him even tighter against her. No ambiguity there.

He groaned in response, savoring the scent of her, the velvet softness of her skin. He wanted to touch her everywhere. Map her body with his fingers, his lips.

How they got naked so fast, he had no idea. They fell onto the bed, a tangle of limbs and molten desire. Her closest nipple drew him like a siren, and he ran his tongue over it. A light suckle caused her to moan and dig her fingers into his back. She was panting when he changed to the other nipple, her magnolia scent mingled with that of her arousal. He grew so hard he ached.

Sam skimmed his hands down her slim throat to both breasts, cupping them as he kissed her again, tangling tongues. His erection pressed against her, and he could feel she was wet and ready for him. He raised his head, looking at the face of the woman he was about to love. Her wanton expression, the swollen lips, the erect nipples nearly undid him.

Then he realized his wallet, and the condoms, were nowhere near the bed.

"Nightstand," she said, reading his mind.

It took only a few moments to collect what he needed and slide it in place. As he did, her sultry gaze followed his every move.

"They don't grow them small in Chicago, do they?"

His laughter filled the room. "God, you're wonderful."

"Prove it," she said, nipping at his collarbone.

Timing his move perfectly, Sam shifted his weight and sank deep within her. From Susan's pleased gasp, he was well on his way to showing her just how wonderful he thought she was.

This was really happening. She'd decided to seize the moment and now he was inside her now, moving, perfectly in tune with what she so desperately needed. As Susan angled her hips, she was pleased when he responded with even deeper thrusts. Then he abruptly shifted his angle and reached that one spot that made her cry out as her first orgasm overtook her in a rush.

But Sam wasn't done. No, not this man. He began varying his rhythm, sometimes stopping completely. She whimpered, digging her fingers into his arms, eager for another release.

"Patience, honey."

She was about to fire back a swear word at his damned patience when he began moving again, his fingers touching her there, stoking the need that made her tighten her inner muscles, trying to break his control. At first, it didn't work. If anything, it took her higher as her belly tightened and her body became hypersensitive. Every movement, every stroke, every breath screamed for release.

"Oh, God!" she cried as she blew apart in an implosion of bright colors and intense sensations. As she writhed beneath him, Sam's control didn't just break, it snapped, like a cable under tremendous pressure. The patient man was gone, consumed by a man who had only one goal: release. Sam thrust faster now, his hands clutching her waist as he drove himself inside her. Closing her eyes, she tangled her legs around his, riding the power behind his passion. When he cried out, she felt tears in her eyes. So much joy. So much happiness. All because of him.

As Susan regained her breath, Sam's arms were still around her, holding her tenderly. When she opened her eyes, he gazed at her with an expression she didn't know how to decipher. It certainly wasn't an "I just got lucky" one. No, far from it.

Sam gently kissed her forehead. "Thank you, dearest lily."

Lily. That's what her name meant in Hebrew. "Thank you, Samuel."

He leveraged himself away from her, though it seemed he did so reluctantly. After discarding the condom, he came back to bed, tucking her up against him. It'd been a long time since she'd felt like this. Cherished. At peace.

Too bad it would end so soon.

7:30 a.m.

A strange *wha wha wha* sound had Sam lurching upward in bed. "What the hell is that?"

"An e-mail from my boss," Susan mumbled.

He rubbed his eyes, barely awake. "Was that the saxophone noise from Charlie Brown?"

"Yup. Seemed appropriate."

Sam lay back down, his heart still pounding. "What time is it?"

"Seven thirty. She gets into the office early. Probably read my report. Now you've done it."

"Me? You sent it," he said, pulling her into his arms.

"You goaded me into it."

"Trust me, in the long run it'll be worth it." He was just about to kiss her and see what other morning activities she might like when the sound went off again.

"See what you've started?" Susan pushed him back. Rolling toward the nightstand, she retrieved her phone. "Don't get up. Maybe this isn't any big deal, and then I'll be back to punish you appropriately."

"Since you're a law-enforcement professional, would this punishment involve handcuffs?" he said, tracing a meandering finger down her spine.

Susan shot him a wicked look over her shoulder that told him cuffs might just be a possibility. When she returned to skimming through the e-mails, her muttering grew louder.

"That doesn't sound good."

"Because it isn't," she said, tossing the phone over her shoulder so it bounced off his chest with a thud. "Take a look while I shower."

Cursing technology, Sam leveraged himself up in bed, leaned against the headboard, and speed-read both e-mails. The first stated that SAC Rhodes expected Susan to be in her office by eight thirty this morning. That meant she'd have to hustle—morning traffic in Atlanta was brutal. Sam clenched his jaw because the second email was a transcript of a complaint filed by Edward Mossman on behalf of WMD.

Citing Susan's friendship with Ms. Wilson's family, Mossman's complaint stated that his law firm was being unfairly targeted by an FBI agent with a personal vendetta., Apparently she was harassing him, compromising the firm's *sterling* reputation—Sam snorted now—and that she had accused the firm of engaging in criminal activities. Curiously, Mossman didn't mention exactly what those were or when she'd made those accusations.

The threat portion of the complaint mentioned a news conference with the local media and a potential multi-million-dollar lawsuit. Mossman went on to name drop like a Hollywood gold digger, citing his firm's relationship with a former governor and two senators. In short, Special Agent Driscoll needed to be severely reprimanded, preferably fired, or all hell would break loose.

"You lying son of a bitch," Sam murmured, wishing the asshole was in front of him right now. He'd risk the assault charge just to tear him apart.

With a shaking hand, he set the phone on Susan's pillow. If his lover was about to face a shitstorm, she needed coffee.

And me to help even the odds.

Susan found Sam in the kitchen, shoeless, hair askew, pouring coffee into her travel mug. How he'd figured out which one of the four she used, she had no clue, but he'd guessed right. He handed it over and then sipped his coffee from her "Because I'm the FBI Agent, That's Why" cup. Despite her roiling gut, she appreciated the gesture and the man who'd made it.

"You read the e-mails?" she asked.

"Yup."

"Any thoughts."

"Nope," he said, frowning. "Well, other than that I have a real desire to rip Mossman's dick off and feed it to him right now."

"I suspect there's a law against that."

"Neutering a rabid dog? Not likely. Bastard deserves to go down, hard."

She knew it was wrong, but she really liked this protective side of Sam. It made her feel appreciated. Loved, even.

"You want backup in this meeting, or would it just make things worse?" he asked, his fingers clenching the cup, white from the pressure.

For a second, her temper flared—did he think she couldn't handle this on her own? Then his tone of voice registered, signaling deep worry.

"You being there will only make it worse. You were right to have me file that report, though Rhodes will suspect I did it just to cover my ass."

"How did Mossman find out you were on the case?"

"Who knows?" She took another long slug of the coffee. "I gotta go. Feel free to hang here if you want, make yourself some breakfast."

Retrieving a piece of notepaper from the counter, she jotted down what he'd need to know. "If you go out, set the alarm. It's pound-sign five. Here's the code if you want to come back in. There's an extra set of keys in the drawer by the sink."

As Sam took the information, the worry in his eyes increased. "You let me know how it goes, okay?"

She tipped up and gave him a kiss on the cheek. "I will."

He set down his cup, wrapped his arms around her, and kissed her. It was a very good kiss, and one she wished didn't have to end.

"For luck," he said. "Just so you know, last night meant a lot to me."

His expression told her he was sincere. "It meant a great deal to me too."

"I screwed up though. Only gave you two orgasms. I'll have to fix that later."

Her face warmed, and for a second, she wished she wasn't an FBI agent who had an angry boss waiting for her. She'd rather stay home in this man's arms. Make love, go for long walks. Make love again. Like other people did.

But she wasn't like other people.

Grabbing her purse and her travel mug, Susan hurried out the door before she blurted out her feelings, ones that even she didn't understand.

Chapter Ten

Susan's Apartment
8:00 a.m.

Sam was too angry to eat, a growing rage that had been hard to hide from Susan. It was a side of him that he didn't often reveal, that primal need to beat someone bloody. As a rookie cop he'd quickly learned that he needed to keep that beast on a choke chain, and usually he was successful. Seeing Susan's fear that her career had just been destroyed made that beast howl for revenge. She might not be his, but he felt like she was, and that's all that mattered.

"This is war, asshole," he murmured. "You went after the wrong woman."

Five new reports sat on the Veritas server, flagged for his attention. He took a sip of coffee and zeroed in on the one from the financial department. It was heavy reading, but he'd minored in economics in college so it all made sense to him. In this case, his hunch had been right: Mossman and Warburg were shunting funds offshore. The issue was whether they'd done it with the IRS's knowledge.

A quick glance at the clock on the mantel told him it was damned early, but he'd take the chance that his friend at the Treasury Department would be in. If his hunch paid off, he'd be helping her career and kicking Mossman in the balls at the same time. Sam hunted through his phone's contacts and found the number.

"Ashman," a light voice answered.

"Devi, it's Sam Marsh."

"Hey, how are you doing? It's been a while. Still rocking away in Chicago?"

"I'm doing well. Currently in Atlanta. How's that new husband of yours? He treating you right?"

"Very much so. Thanks for the wedding present. A year's supply of Kona coffee? Do you know how much we adore you every morning?"

He laughed. "I called because I might have something for you. Don't know if it's real or not, but it's worth checking out."

"You've yet to give me a dud."

By the end of the call, he could feel Devi's excitement. She lived to find people who hid money offshore to avoid paying Uncle Sam his fair share, and he'd just given her a very tasty morsel to chew on.

"I'll let you know what I find. Should have an answer fairly quickly. My hunch is that they didn't bother to tell us about this cash," she said.

"Mine too. Happy hunting," he said. "Please send my regards to your husband."

"I shall. I'll call you soon, one way or another."

One time bomb ticking away.

He opened the report on Mossman's time as a vice cop. Now, it was time to lay a few more.

Atlanta FBI Field Office
8:30 a.m.

Susan knocked on the door, trying not to panic and failing. As she saw it, she was screwed. Influential lawyer threatening to call in the big dogs? Only one way this could go. Rhodes would automatically seek to keep the heat off the office, and by extension, herself. Susan, as the troublemaker, was another matter.

"Come in!" her boss called out.

Mentally girding herself for the worst, Susan reluctantly pushed open the door. She'd been in this office more often than she preferred. In fact, the only way she wanted to be here was for a five-second "Good job on that case, Agent Driscoll," and then take off. That hadn't happened yet—despite the fact that she'd helped save Atlanta from a terrorist—and she wasn't holding her breath that it ever would.

As expected, Special Agent in Charge Maxine Rhodes was behind her desk, settled in for the day's work. She was in her mid-fifties, the last twenty-five of which had been with the FBI. From what Susan had heard, she'd married and divorced twice. The job was a relationship killer, for sure.

When Susan's former and much beloved boss had died of a heart attack while jogging on a beach in St. Maarten, it'd been Rhodes who was sent to take his place. Most of the agents in the office got along with her. Susan was the exception.

Ms. Rhodes's tailored navy suit jacket hung from the back of her chair, her white blouse pristine, as always. Her silver-streaked black hair was pulled back into a ponytail and even the hair band was navy. No rings, no watch, small pearl earrings. As if the only colorful thing in her life was her job.

Susan glanced down at her own attire and stifled a wince. She wasn't dressed much differently, and she wasn't sure what that said about her, either.

Rhodes looked up at her. "Right on time," she said.

Susan sat in the chair in front of her boss's desk, feeling like she'd just been sent to the principal's office.

Her superior removed her reading glasses, placing them on the desk. Then eyed her. "Found any terrorists lurking in our fair city recently? Perhaps at the grocery store or the local delicatessen?"

This level of snark was new, uncharacteristic even, so Susan chose not to get pissed as quickly as usual. "They're pretty thin on the ground right now."

"Good. That's a blessing." Rhodes gestured at the papers stacked in front of her. "This morning, I have on my desk your report and a complaint. Let's start with the former."

"Okay, but at this point I want to reiterate that at no time during my inquiries did I go anywhere near the law firm, nor did I mention that I was with the Bureau. The only people who know I'm an agent are Detective Hall, his partner, Mr. Marsh, and the victim's family."

"You told the APD detectives you were with the Bureau?"

"No. Pat already knew. We . . . dated a few years back."

Rhodes leaned back in her chair. "I see. So you've been doing this investigation on your own time?"

"Yes."

"Using Bureau resources?"

"No, none," Susan said, shaking her head for emphasis. "This is all on me. Well, except for Sam's . . . Mr. Marsh's help."

Her boss quirked an eyebrow. "Yes, we'll get back to him in a moment."

That comment made Susan even more uncomfortable. It was like waiting for an anvil to drop on your head, knowing there was no way to duck it. You just knew it was going to hurt like a bitch.

"Any idea why Edward Mossman decided to file a complaint about you?" her boss asked, eyes riveted on her.

"Other than he's a complete dick?" she said, before she could edit her words.

To her surprise, Rhodes actually nodded in agreement. "Besides that."

"I don't know. We made sure that Sam went to their office, instead of me. He didn't mention the FBI in any way, because we didn't want Mossman or his cronies thinking this was an official investigation."

"I'm fully aware that some of your actions were to obtain plausible deniability should I go on the warpath," Rhodes said.

No reason to lie. "That too."

"This Mr. Marsh, the former homicide detective from Chicago. He on the level?"

"Completely," Susan replied without hesitation. "One thing I didn't mention in the report: He works for Veritas. He was here on vacation and witnessed Treina's shooting. It was pure coincidence he was at the scene."

"Really?" Rhodes replied, tenting her fingers in front of her now. Her cell phone vibrated and she gave it a quick look, then ignored whoever was calling. "Mossman know he's with them?"

"Not that I'm aware. Sam didn't tell WMD he worked for Veritas when he was at their office. The business card he gave them was for a dummy investigative firm. That didn't keep Mossman from calling Sam's supposed 'boss' about how abusive he'd been, and threatening to have his PI license lifted."

"So you're not the only one he's complaining about." Susan shook her head. "I've done more research into Veritas since our run-in with them in the swamp," Rhodes continued. "Did you know they love to jump into things that are none of their business? That the man who heads up the company is an international criminal?"

Her temper stirred. "Yes, I do now. With all due respect, ma'am, they were there for me when it counted. Since I was down there on my own, if I hadn't had their backup, I'd have been buried next to that other field agent after Ellers forced me to drink his homemade ricin."

"Is that how Agent Vandermeer died?" Rhodes asked, quieter now.

Susan nodded. "Britelli got a copy of the autopsy report from the Brunswick office." She didn't need to tell her boss that the man's death would have been agonizingly painful. "Yes, Crispin Wilder was an arms dealer. I know he isn't now, and that he threw valuable resources at the situation that saved lives."

"Ellers should have gone to trial, not been killed," Rhodes retorted.

"That would have been great, but he died trying to escape with a helicopter full of weapons and ricin. Frankly, I'm thrilled he's dead. I just wish I'd had the chance to kill the bastard myself."

Her boss sighed as if she'd expected to hear just that. "How familiar are you with Warburg, Mossman and Day?"

"Not that much," Susan replied. *Other than the fact that they want to destroy my career.*

"Well, they're a tank full of sharks. At least Warburg and Mossman are. I don't know that much about Day. I have colleagues in the attorney general's office who have shared a few tales over drinks. 'Weapons of Mass Destruction' is what they call them."

Rhodes actually went drinking with colleagues?

"They file a flurry of motions to slow roll the judicial process, they bully witnesses, they question the professional integrity of the law-enforcement officers who worked the cases. They've been known to use blackmail, as well as physical and financial threats to keep their clients out of jail. It's why anyone with deep pockets goes to them when they get arrested."

"Would they go so far as to try to kill an employee?"

Rhodes nodded. "I wouldn't put it past them. It all depends on what Ms. Wilson saw while she worked there. I notice you mentioned this woman is pregnant. Any idea who the father is?"

Susan shook her head. "The family doesn't know either."

Rhodes took a deep breath, as if weighing several options. Susan suspected none of them were good.

"Here's the thing," the woman began. "You and I are never going to see eye to eye if you keep doing your lone wolf thing. We go about the job entirely differently, and since I'm your boss, I have to answer to the higher-ups when you do something stupid."

She began to protest, but was stopped by a raised hand.

"You were smart to file this report, because it would have gone a lot worse for you if you hadn't. However, because a complaint has been filed, I have to move carefully. Officially, I'm going to tell you to stop doing whatever you're doing, or you're on suspension pending a disciplinary hearing."

It took a moment for Susan to parse what the woman had said. "And *unofficially?*"

"Find out what's going on here, because this sure as hell stinks. I need concrete evidence of criminal behavior. If that includes contract murder and attempted murder, so much the better. I'd love nothing more than to nail these bastards' balls to the barn door."

What the hell?

It took Susan a moment to catch up. "Ah, do I have permission to use Bureau resources?"

"Yes, but keep it quiet. Britelli can help, but not in any way that puts him in jeopardy. If this goes bad, he needs cover."

Unlike me. Because she'd be the sacrificial goat. "Understood."

"As far as the real world is concerned, I just read you the riot act and you're still on leave. No matter what, even if nothing is happening, send me detailed updates. Those might ensure you have a job when this is all over." Rhodes waved her toward the door. "Oh, and watch your back. These guys play rough."

"Yeah, they do just that."

Especially if they were willing to execute a pregnant woman.

Susan was still processing what had happened with her boss as she logged into her desktop computer. Now she had access to Bureau resources, which were formidable. Even better, she hadn't been told to avoid Veritas. That was a surprise. Maybe Rhodes had learned something after the Ellers case.

"You still one of us?" Britelli asked as he joined her, his face full of concern.

"Not canned yet."

Joe stood just a bit over six feet, was solidly built, and had thick, dark, curly hair. Susan had always thought hair that gorgeous was wasted on a guy. His wife, Sophia, didn't agree. He nodded as he sat in the chair on the other side of the desk.

After she'd finished telling him how it'd played out with their boss, he finally cracked a smile. "That I didn't expect. What's my role in this?" he asked.

"Nothing overt. Rhodes wants you to have cover if this blows up in my face. But if you could contact the FAA and see if WMD chartered a flight to Colorado this last week, I'd appreciate it. We need to find the missing partner."

"Can do."

"Oh, and while I was in with the boss, Pat texted me. The crime scene techs lifted prints off the door handle of the cab and Treina's purse, as well as partials off the brick in the alley, and at the cabbie's apartment. The owner of those prints is one Rich Valens. Pat says he's got an impressive rap sheet. They're issuing an arrest warrant."

Joe nodded his approval. "Good. Now here's the deal, partner. No matter what happens here, don't go all Lone Ranger on me. You pulled that shit in the swamp, and I'm still pissed about it."

She smiled for the first time since she'd arrived at work, knowing his grouchiness was that of a concerned friend.

"I promise I won't make that mistake again. Provided you stop trying to pair me up with one of your Italian cousins."

"Hey, they're all great guys," Joe replied with a big smile. "Well, except for Bernie. He's a putz. Can't all be like me." He rapped his knuckles on her desk as he stood. "Keep yourself alive, you hear?" he said, then left her to do her work.

After firing off a text to Sam, letting him know she was still employed, she put a call in to Pat. It was time to start pulling the pieces of this puzzle together, so when it was all over, the right people were in jail. If one of those happened to be Edward Mossman, so much the better.

Susan's Apartment
Noon

Though Susan's text had indicated all was well on her end—Sam couldn't wait to hear why that was the case—he found he was in no hurry to leave her apartment. He should find another hotel room, but something wouldn't let him budge off the sofa. That something was Susan. Even though she wasn't here, he was surrounded by her and it made him feel good.

His parents had talked about that kind of thing, how from the moment they'd met there'd been a deep connection. That had proved awkward since his mom was engaged to someone else. Fortunately, his folks had worked out exactly what that soul-level connection meant—she'd broken her engagement—and they'd been happily married for forty years.

But what did that have to do with Susan? Was it just the situation that was causing this intense attraction, or was it something else?

Sam heard the sound of someone at the front door. As it swung open, Susan called out to him and he smiled.

He rose off the sofa. "Looking fine, Agent Driscoll."

"I was hoping you'd hang around," she said, setting her purse on the kitchen counter. Her suit coat went on a chair and then her shoes came off, one by one.

Sam walked around the sofa and leaned back against it, enjoying every little movement. Her welcoming smile, the brightness in her eyes, how she seemed less tense now, more . . . alive. He hoped he'd contributed to all that.

When she turned toward him, he opened his arms and she walked right into them. "Missed you," he said, kissing her neck as her breasts pressed against his chest.

As his hands slid down her thighs, then rucked up her skirt, she ran her hands up into his hair, pulling him in for a kiss, telling him his advances were more than welcome. They'd just sunk into a deep French kiss, one that promised more time in bed, when her phone began to sing some Italian song.

He growled. "It can't be anyone important."

She lightly banged her head against his chest in despair. "Yes, it is. It's my partner."

When he reluctantly let her loose Susan hustled into the kitchen.

"Hi, Joe." She shot Sam a steamy glance. "Your timing really sucks."

"You're supposed to be working, lady, not getting a little," Joe replied.

"Says the guy who's been known to slip home for a nooner with the wife," she said.

"At least you got the timing right," he jested.

"So what's going on?"

"Why don't you put us on speaker so Mr. PI can hear this, too."

She did as he'd asked. "Go for it."

"The FAA called back. WMD's corporate jet left for Centennial, Colorado, on Monday, then returned late that evening. One passenger outbound, a Robinson Day. No passengers on the way back to Atlanta."

"So he *is* in Colorado."

"Not any longer. The jet returned to Centennial late last night. It left Colorado this morning and is scheduled to land at PDK at about one."

She did a quick glance at the clock on the mantel and found it was just a little after noon. "This is great news, Joe."

"Good enough news to forgive me for the cock blocking?"

"You're forgiven. We'll pick Day up, see what his story is. I'll keep you in the loop."

"Sounds good. Oh, Mr. PI?"

"Yeah?" Sam called back as he pulled on his shoes.

"You treat her right or you're a maggot-ridden corpse, you got it?"

Sam didn't even blink. "Understood. But if I screw up, Susan will snuff me long before you get a chance."

"Either way, you're dead, so just keep that in mind. Talk to you later, Suz."

"Good*bye*, Joe." She cut the connection. "Sorry about my partner."

"No sweat. I'd be saying the same thing if I were him."

She nodded. "We'll need to leave in ten to make the airport in time. Bring your computer along. We might need it."

As Susan headed to the bathroom, Sam's lengthy sigh

accompanied her. He was as sexually frustrated as she was.

While she fixed her makeup, she had no choice but to come to a few conclusions. It was obvious that Sam was the kind of guy she'd been hoping to find. He was well mannered, fiercely honest, very intelligent, and one helluva lover. The kind of man she could take to family dinners and never worry that he was going to embarrass her in front of her folks.

He understood her crazy work schedule and that she liked her private time. The kind of man that would make her look forward to her weekends off, because instead of loneliness they'd be filled with fun, laughter, and many, many body-shaking orgasms.

Why couldn't you live in Atlanta?

That would be perfect. Of course, the universe wasn't going to be that accommodating.

As if she'd summoned him, Sam appeared at the bathroom door, all dressed and ready. "So where is this airport?"

After running a brush through her hair, she tucked it into a loose bun. "DeKalb-Peachtree Airport is north of here, in Chamblee. It's a smaller field, handles corporate jets and fixed-wing aircraft so they don't clog up Hartsfield-Jackson. It won't be too bad to get there this time of day."

"How do you think we should approach this guy?" Sam asked.

"Carefully. Nothing indicates he's on Team Sleaze with his partners, but that doesn't mean he isn't."

"So far, Day's background check is clean. Nothing that makes my nose twitch. Curiously, Ms. Ott has recently paid off her house and bought a new Lexus, but those events occurred shortly after WMD paid their annual bonuses, so she may have scored heavily there." He leaned on the doorjamb. "Oh, and I sicced a Treasury agent on Mossman."

She set down her mascara. "Really?"

"Yeah. He fucking pissed me off with what he did to you. Time for him to learn doing shit like that has consequences."

Susan was momentarily stunned by his coarse language, an indicator of just how angry he was on her behalf.

"The Treasury? That's hardcore, Sam."

"Mossman tried to nuke your career, so I want to nuke him in return. He made it easy; Veritas found that both he and Warburg have serious cash reserves offshore. I'm willing to bet my entire 401K balance that neither of them bothered to tell Uncle Sam about that cash."

"Of course they didn't. Don't you know, the rules don't apply to their kind."

His usual genial smile turned predatory. "They're about to find out that's not the case."

Chapter Eleven

DeKalb-Peachtree Airport
12:58 p.m.

"The plane you're looking for will be landing right after the King Air," the man at the charter office explained.

"Great. Thanks," Susan replied. She'd pretty much figured that out by listening to the control tower chatter, but it was nice to have it confirmed.

She and Sam watched with nervous anticipation as the King landed, followed by a sleek corporate jet.

"Wonder how much one of those puppies costs," she said.

"A lot," he replied. "That's a Cessna Citation. Stripped down, they start at roughly four million. All tricked out they can reach twenty-six million. That's why most companies charter them. Cheaper than owning their own."

She stared at him. "How do you know all that?"

"I do a lot of research, so I learn weird, impractical stuff. I'm the guy you want on your team on Trivia Night."

"You are a constant source of amazement, you know that?"

"Good. I like keeping you off balance."

"No problem there."

The instant the stairs were lowered, Robinson Day exited the aircraft, phone to his ear. He had a computer case hanging from a shoulder and rolled along a small carry-on suitcase behind him. Day was a tall man, well over six feet, distinguished looking with a solid build. Kind of handsome in his own way, with ash-blond hair cut to just the right length.

His expression seemed distant, as if he was going through the motions. As he drew closer, the dark circles under his eyes became noticeable, as did the way his right hand clenched his phone.

"What do you think?" Sam asked.

"I think we have one worried guy. Might be because he's a co-conspirator and knows the shit is hitting the fan. Or not. We're about to find out."

As soon as Day entered the building, Susan intercepted him, calling out his name. The attorney came to a halt, frowning.

"Yes, I'm headed to the office," he said, in reply to a question over the phone. "I have some personal things to do first." He ended the call and stared at the pair of them. "Yes, I'm Rob Day. Who are you?"

"Special Agent Susan Driscoll, FBI," she said, holding up her badge and ID. "This is Sam Marsh."

Day stared at her ID for a few seconds, then sighed. "You're wanting to talk to me about the firm, right?"

That had been easy. "Yes, we are. But first, I need to know if you're Treina Wilson's fiancé?"

"I am. Why?" Then the color drained from his face. "Oh, God. Did something happen to her?"

Susan traded a look with Sam, then nodded. "Yes, you could say that."

Rob Day learned exactly what had happened to his fiancée in the charter company's breakroom, which at least afforded them some privacy. He held up fairly well as Susan told him that Treina was in the hospital, that she and the baby were doing okay. That they were expected to recover.

It wasn't until she told him exactly how the woman he loved had been injured that the man lost it. Hanging his head, Day's shoulders began to heave. Then he openly sobbed. If Sam had been in his place, he'd have been doing the same.

Susan hunted around and then set a box of tissues on the table in front of him. Day grabbed some and crushed them in his hand.

"Why was she in a cab? She has her own car." He knuckled away his tears, forgetting the tissues. "Jesus, who the hell shoots a pregnant woman?" he demanded.

"We thought maybe you could tell us."

Day's shock was joined by anger. "Those bastards! I never thought they'd go this far. I should have known something was up when LeeAnn died."

"LeeAnn?" Sam asked.

"LeeAnn Hunter was my executive secretary. Heidi's her replacement." Day shook his head. "I mentioned it to the cops at the time, but they said it was just an 'unfortunate' accident." He sighed. "Maybe it was."

"How did she die?"

"She was struck by a car after she'd walked her son to school. Hit-and-run driver."

Susan winced at that. "Do you think Treina knew something that might have led to her attack?"

Day nodded. "My partners are as crooked as they come. I didn't realize it when I bought into the company, but once I was there, I knew things weren't right." Suddenly he was on his feet. "God, she probably thinks I don't love her anymore. I tried calling, but she never answered. Look, I'll tell you everything, but I have to see Treina now. "

"The doctors have her sedated, so she isn't aware that you haven't been there," Susan replied. "We'll take you to the hospital to see her, but then we'd like to sit down with you and the detectives in charge of the murder investigation. We've got a lot of questions."

The man wasn't listening, already headed to the door that led to the parking lot. Fortunately, Sam was able to get in front of him, giving a quick scan of the premises. There'd been four vehicles in the parking lot when they arrived, and that number hadn't changed. Three sat near the entrance; another was parked at the far end of the lot.

"My car is down here," Day said, pointing at the one sitting by itself. He'd forgotten his suitcase, which luckily, Susan had realized. She rolled it up next to him and he claimed it.

"WMD will know when he was to arrive," Sam said quietly to ensure that the man in question didn't hear him. "Be careful."

"We will be." She handed Sam her car keys. "Can you follow us? He's not in any shape to be behind the wheel, so I'll drive."

Though Sam agreed with her assessment, he really wanted to be the one with Day in case someone felt the need to ensure the attorney never made it back to his office.

As they walked away, she claimed the distraught man's keys. "Don't worry, we'll get this sorted out. Treina will be happy to know you're home with her."

Susan put her hand on the man's arm for support, then shook her head at something he said. The farther they were away from Sam, the more his neck twitched. He did another three-sixty. Same cars, nothing new.

If he wanted Day dead, how would he do it? Airplane accident? No, that moment had passed. Sniper? A quick check proved there wasn't a good location to set up a position. Bomb? There'd been plenty of time to place one. But where?

Day's car.

Still talking, Susan raised her hand to click the remote start button.

He might be wrong, but if he wasn't . . .

"Susan!" Sam called out, sprinting toward them. "Wait!"

When she heard Sam call her name, she began to turn. It was only then that Susan saw the late-model Chevy pulling up on the opposite side of the fence that bordered the road. As the passenger-side window rolled down, she shouted, "Watch out!"

Without thinking, she shoved Day to the ground, covering him with her body. Somehow, as she landed, her fingers hit the start button on the remote and the car dutifully honked in response.

Then it erupted in a fireball. The resounding explosion shook the earth beneath them, and a second or two later, the concussion wave rolled over them, causing gravel to sandblast them like hail. Once it had passed, Susan blinked her eyes to try to clear them.

Unable to see the Chevy through the cloud of dust, she tapped Day on the shoulder where he lay next to her. "You hurt?" He shook his head as he rose up on his elbows, his navy suit covered with grime, right cheek scraped from the gravel. Before he could reply, gunfire erupted, bullets kicking up dirt around them.

"Move!" she shouted, grabbing him and pulling him to his feet. As they ran toward the nearest car to take cover, there were more shots, and then the sound of tires squealing.

"Sam?" she called out, her gun drawn now.

No reply. Her mind foresaw blood and death. "Sam!"

"I'm here," he called back, his form appearing out of the dust cloud. "You two okay?"

She heaved a massive sigh of relief. "Yeah, we're good. You?"

"Yeah, okay," he said.

Susan would never forget his expression as he walked toward her, a mix of unbridled fear, profound anger, and all-encompassing relief. It was the look of someone who would be devastated if this day had ended differently.

All those emotions mirrored hers exactly.

Unnerved at how frightened she'd been for his safety, she fell back on her dark humor. "Man, what some people will do for a parking place."

Sam had just put his gun in his shoulder holster, and now he and Day were both staring at her like she was mad. It took a second or two, then Sam broke out in laughter, leading to deep belly laughs. Day didn't join him, but kept staring.

"Cop humor," she said, shrugging. "It's how we roll."

"Ohhkay," the attorney replied, but he didn't sound convinced.

When Sam finally stopped laughed, he touched her cheek so gently, not seeming to care if anyone witnessed this personal moment between them. "You are amazing, Special Agent

Driscoll."

"So are you, Mr. Marsh," she said. She glanced over at the other man. "Rob, you still good?"

Day gave a stiff nod, then sent his attention to his burning car, which was adding its share of toxic black smoke to Atlanta's pollution problem. "I can't believe they tried to kill me. You know, I just made the last payment on that thing."

"Of course you did. It always works that way." Susan eyed her partner now. "Still think remote starts are a gimmick?"

"Best invention ever," he replied. "I'll insist on having them in all my cars from now on."

"Did you get a look at the guy?"

Sam shook his head. "No rear tag, either."

The charter office manager jogged up now, his breath whistling. "I called the cops and fire department."

As if in response came the sound of sirens, multiple ones. As they walked back to the office to await the cops, Sam lagged behind them, making a call. To whom, Susan wasn't sure. Once Day was tucked safely inside, she had some calls to make herself, starting with her boss.

Emory University Hospital
2:30 p.m.

By the time Rob Day reached the hospital to see his betrothed, the man had regained his equilibrium, which was remarkable. He was the consummate gentleman as he introduced himself to Treina's mother and sister, apologizing for not meeting them earlier, and for his appearance. Then he stood by his fiancée's hospital bed, stroking her hand, and wept again.

He's a good man. Quiet, thoughtful, but likely a bear when crossed. Susan bet this guy was hell on wheels in the courtroom. Treina was going to need that strength if she ever went to court to testify against Valens and whoever was pulling his strings.

Knowing Day wasn't going anywhere soon, Susan backed out of the room. Her partner was waiting for her just outside the door.

"Shit, you're all chewed up," Joe said, pointing at her face and arms. "Next time, remember to wear a helmet and leather."

Susan chuckled. "No next time. This one sucked enough."

"From what I heard, it was pretty damned close," he said, sobering.

She shrugged, which made her back ache. "What's Rhodes's take on this?"

"The boss lady is furious. She might not be fond of you, but that doesn't give any asshole the right to try to incinerate an FBI agent, and a potential witness. At least not on her watch."

"Huh." Susan angled her head toward the room. "Can you bring Rob to wherever we're meeting? He refuses to go to our office and leave his fiancée behind. He'll be more cooperative here."

"Will do."

After a nurse told her where to find Pat and her PI, she headed for a restroom. The face that looked back at her in the mirror was in better shape than it felt. She'd gotten worse road rash when she wiped out on her bike when she was eight. Susan cleaned up the blood as best she could. No real point in fixing her makeup.

Leaning against the sink, she took a deep breath, compartmentalizing how close she'd come to dying today. Down the line, she'd pull that issue out, examine it, maybe even give into a couple minutes of full-body shaking. But right now, it was time to figure out why someone wanted Robinson Day and Treina Wilson dead.

Sam and Pat were talking quietly when she entered the meeting room; in fact, they seemed to be completely at ease with each other. She wasn't exactly sure when that had changed, but it was a welcome one. Then it hit her: Since Sam had called Veritas while they were waiting for the cops to arrive, she'd bet his call right after the blast had been to her ex-boyfriend.

Because the last thing you ever wanted to do was hear the news secondhand.

Before she could join them, the smell of fresh coffee caught her nose and she veered off to collect some.

"How's Day doing?" Sam asked.

"Realizing just how much his life has gone to hell in the last few days," Susan replied. "Seeing Treina helped some."

"That, I wouldn't doubt. We have a couple witnesses at PDK who saw the Chevy both coming and going," Pat said. "They ID'd a mug shot; it was Valens."

"So he's like this all-purpose assassin?" Susan said.

"No. His priors show he's smart enough to pull off a shooting, but rigging up a bomb? My guess is that he didn't build it—he just attached it to the car."

"Then he hung around just to watch it go boom?"

"Hey, nothing but reruns on the TV, what else is he going to do?" Pat replied.

"Not funny."

The door behind them opened, revealing Day, who seemed more composed now.

"The coffee's fresh," Sam said, gesturing.

"No, thanks," he replied, pulling out a chair and sinking into it. Joe was right behind him, but remained by the door, pulling guard duty. Susan nodded her appreciation.

"Bill's watching the lady," Joe announced. "He'll scare anyone off who's the least bit suspicious. Makes it easier that she's in the ICU."

At Sam's puzzled look, Susan explained, "Bill was a fullback for the Denver Broncos. He's huge. Anyone goes after Treina, they're small bite-sized bits."

"Works for me." He turned his attention to Day now. "How's your fiancée doing?"

"Treina's still pretty much out of it," Day replied, "but the docs say she'll be fully awake by tomorrow, and they'll move her to a regular room then."

"Thank God," Susan murmured.

"I think she knew I was there. It was weird, though. She

kept saying 'heart' over and over, like I'd know what she meant."

That didn't make any sense to Susan, either. She laid her phone on the table and clicked the record button. She'd already discussed recording this interview, and Day was good with it. After stating the time, date, location, and the people in the room, she began.

"Mr. Day, why do you think someone is trying to kill you and Treina Wilson?"

The man rubbed his eyes, weary. "It has something to do with my partners at the law firm."

"That firm being Warburg, Mossman and Day, PC, correct?" she asked, just for clarification on the recording.

"Yes." He took a deep inhalation as if preparing himself. "I bought into the firm a little over eighteen months ago. Seemed like a great career move. The deal we made was that I would handle all the civil litigation cases and they'd handle the criminal ones.

"Something changed about eight months ago. First off, Ed took on the Neager case, the one involving human trafficking. At the time, I couldn't believe he'd risk our firm's reputation over that guy, but it wasn't my call. I voiced my concerns, and Ed said Neager was innocent." He paused, uneasy. "Sorry, can I still have some coffee?"

Sam rose and brought him some. After a long sip, Day set the cup down, staring at it as if he couldn't handle looking them in the eyes.

"LeeAnn Hunter, my executive secretary at the time, received an e-mail that wasn't intended for her. It was confirmation of a wire transfer in the amount of two million dollars to an account in the Caymans. She called me and asked what this was, and I told her I didn't know. So she followed up on it with Ed's secretary, Gail . . .Ott, and was told it was a retainer. That it wasn't her concern."

"Why send a retainer out of the country?" Susan asked.

"Exactly my question. I intended to ask Ed about it when I returned to the office, but then LeeAnn died and Gail took over as my secretary until I hired Heidi. Frankly, I was so shocked at LeeAnn's death that I forgot to follow up about the money."

"Are you sure Ms. Hunter's death was truly an accident?"

"That's what the cops said." He looked at Pat now. "Might want to look at that again."

"Already being done," he replied. "What happened next?"

"When the prosecutors dropped the Neager case, I thought that was the end of it. During one of our partner meetings, I told them that I was not happy this firm was representing perverts. Up to that point, Warburg had been nothing but an old Southern gentleman. That all changed. He asked if I was 'happy' at WMD. Said I needed to learn how to be a team player. It was the most condescending thing I've ever experienced. Then it got worse."

"How?"

"He asked about my sisters and my mom, wondering how they were doing. He even mentioned my two young nieces. Asked if they liked the school they attended. Wanted to know if the eldest had made it into the play she'd auditioned for. The threat was there. Cross him or Mossman, and someone in my family was going to get hurt."

"Shit," Pat said. "You sure this guy isn't mobbed up?"

"I never saw any evidence of that, but who knows? With LeeAnn dead, Treina took over some of her duties until I hired Heidi. Tre and I found ourselves working a very complicated tax-evasion case that involved late hours and, well . . . " A broad smile filled his face, transforming him. "Now we're engaged and we're going to have a baby."

"You're a very lucky man," Sam said, his eyes shifting to Susan at that moment.

"I am. Treina's wonderful. I made a mistake, though. I told her what Warburg had said about my family and it made her furious. She said we had to stop them or someone else would get hurt. Little did I know it would be her."

"Was Treina a warning for you to back off?" Susan asked.

"Maybe. With what could be going on there, we didn't let anyone know we were dating, or engaged. Treina swore she'd have what we needed to go to the FBI in another week or two. I didn't want her involved in this, but she can be . . . stubborn. She said she'd be fine, that she had someone inside the firm helping her get what we needed. She wouldn't back down."

"Any idea who was helping her?" Sam asked and Day shook his head. "You think she found the evidence she wanted?"

"I have no idea. The trip to Colorado came out of nowhere and Warburg insisted I had to make it, rather than one of the junior attorneys. That was unusual, and I hated the thought of being away from her. When I arrived at the client's ranch, which was in the middle of absolute nowhere, his staff told me he was in Salt Lake City at a meeting and would be home in a day or two. That wasn't the plan when I left Atlanta.

"When I couldn't reach Treina after a couple days, I called for the jet to pick me up. Deep down, I knew something had happened." Day sighed. "We should have been straight with her parents right up front, but she was afraid of what would happen if the firm found out we were dating."

"Did you contact the office and ask about her?"

"Yes, I talked to Gail. She said Treina was home sick with a cold. She never said a word about her being shot," he replied, his voice cold now. "Not a goddamned word."

"Ott told me you *did* know, but I thought it odd you hadn't contacted the family to see if they needed anything. Now we know why," Sam said.

"Why would Treina meet someone at Secrets and Lies?" Susan asked.

Day shrugged. "She went to a birthday party there once, for a friend of hers." He rubbed his face now, which made the gravel burns even redder. "How do we stop them?" he murmured. "Because they won't give up until we're both dead."

"Heart," Sam said quietly, as if to himself. He looked over at Susan. "If Treina had the evidence she needed, I doubt she would have taken it with her to the club, so it has to be in her apartment somewhere."

Nodding, she stated the time the recording ended, then attached it to an e-mail and sent copies to Pat and her boss.

"Mr. Day, would you like to go back to your fiancée's room, or to a safe location for a few hours so you can rest?" Joe asked.

Day rose. "I want to be with Treina. I can never make up for what happened to her, but I can let her know I'll never leave her in danger again."

As they walked out into the hallway, Joe caught Susan's arm, leaning closer. "Forgot to tell you earlier that the heat's starting to build. Rhodes received 'concerned' calls from two senators and a congressman about a half hour after the bombing wondering why the FBI was harassing a prestigious firm like WMD."

"What did she tell them?"

"That anytime anyone tried to kill an FBI agent, it didn't matter who called to complain, the Bureau wasn't going to back off. And if they had any sense, they might want to take cover because that investigation could reach all the way to Washington."

Susan whistled under her breath. "There are times I actually admire that woman, but please don't tell her that."

Joe smirked. "My silence will cost you coffee for a week."

"With your addiction to caffeine? I'm so bankrupt."

"Ha! Your wallet, not mine."

"Any particular place we should look in the apartment, Mr. Day?" Sam asked.

The man shook his head, looking haggard now. "Treina's clever, so I have no idea where she'd hide something if she didn't want it to be found."

"Looks like we're hunting for the Holy Grail," Susan said.

"Worked for Indiana Jones. Might work for us," Sam replied.

"You do remember what happened to the Nazis in that movie?"

"Oh yeah. One of the best parts. Great special effects."

She groaned and headed down the hall, the PI in tow.

Chapter Twelve

Treina's Apartment
4:40 p.m.

Stairwells were the worst. The psychiatrist Sam had seen after his partner's death had said it was post-traumatic stress that made his pulse race and his breath grow labored every time he was in one. The memory of climbing the narrow stairs in the decrepit apartment building, reaching the landing, and then watching his partner be blown away. Then being shot himself. No matter what the shrink said, giving the panic a label didn't help one damned bit.

Once again, that fear tried to gain control of him. Sweat formed on Sam's brow, his hands shook, each breath became tighter. He could almost feel the impact of the bullets in his chest. In the past he'd tried counting stairs to keep himself distracted, then discarded that as stupid. What if he was counting away and a suspect came out of an apartment and shot him? He'd be dead before he took the next step.

So over time he'd invented his own way of coping: He became hypervigilant. Every little detail was evaluated, from the lighting, to the condition of the steps, the railing, whether it needed a coat of paint. He was doing that now as they ascended to Treina's apartment, noting that one of the handrails was more worn than the other.

Of course, Susan noticed. "You okay?"

"No. I hate apartment stairwells."

"Because of your partner?"

Sam issued a single nod, trying to keep his mind on their surroundings. To his relief, she didn't ask him any further questions, allowing him to concentrate.

Susan unlocked the apartment door, pushing it open with a foot, her gun out. Then looked over at Sam. He carried her backup weapon—the cops had taken his gun as evidence after he'd shot at Valens's car. Once they were inside, they both came to a halt at the sound of an angry voice coming from the back of the apartment.

"Dammit, bitch, where the hell is it? It's gotta be here somewhere."

"Bedroom?" she mouthed. Sam nodded.

They made their way cautiously down the hallway as the intruder kept talking to himself, complaining about how he couldn't find shit in this place. Ironic, because if this *was* Valens, he'd made the mess in the first place. Given the noise he was generating, it was unlikely he'd heard their entry. If they were careful, they could snag him without shots being fired.

Susan quickly searched the first room off the hallway, ensuring it was empty, and took a position just inside the door. Sam went a little farther down the hall to the next room—the nursery—and slipped inside. As he stepped backward, he bumped into something. Looking down, he spied a small can of gasoline that hadn't been here before. He shifted it out of the way so he didn't accidentally knock it over.

When he snuck a peek toward the back bedroom, a familiar scraggly blond paced by the doorway. Sam smiled. Rich Valens had actually returned to the scene of one of his crimes. He still wore his jacket, which meant he was probably armed. Sam ducked back out of sight just as the man's cell phone rang.

"What? No, I haven't found it," Valens growled. The sound of something being kicked came from the bedroom now. "You didn't tell me I was icing a fed. Are you fucking crazy?" Someone argued back, but Sam couldn't tell if the voice was male or female. "Yeah, I'll torch this place, but we're fucking done, you got it? I'm not going to jail for you, asshole."

Valens moved down the hall, stuffing his phone away in a pocket. As he entered the nursery, Sam shifted his gun to his left hand and swung his right fist at the guy. The blow connected, sending Valens careening back into the hallway where he bashed into the wall. Before he could regain his senses, Susan had the murderer turned, his face mashed into the wall, cuffs on one wrist, then the other. She retrieved his gun from his pocket and handed it to Sam for safekeeping.

"What a team," Sam said, holstering his own weapon. "That was sweet, even if my hand is going to bruise."

"Less paperwork than shooting this sorry piece of crap," Susan replied. As she read Valens his rights, he kept staring at her over his shoulder. When she asked if he understood those rights, he mumbled, "Yes." Then something seemed to click. "Oh, hell. It's you. The chick at the airport."

"That's Special Agent Chick to you," she replied. "Congratulations. You've earned yourself a primo chance to receive Georgia's death penalty. Personally, I will rejoice the day you are put down."

Sam leaned against the doorjamb. "Just out of curiosity, are you named after the musician?"

"What musician?"

"Never mind. I don't know why I bothered to ask."

"I want an attorney," Valens insisted. "I know my rights."

They all said that. "Which lawyer do you want?" Susan asked. "Mossman? Warburg? Or maybe Mr. Day. You know, the guy whose fiancée you shot? His *pregnant* fiancée? Yeah, I bet he'd do a damned fine job for you."

Valens shook his head. "I didn't know the Black chick was knocked up. They didn't tell me. They just said—" He realized he was rambling, so he closed his mouth and glared at them.

Now he gets smart.

Once the cops had hauled Valens and his gas can away, they resumed their search for what everyone seemed to want and no one could find. Susan tried to think like a late-twenties paralegal. Treina would be very comfortable on computers and smartphones, less likely to keep whatever she'd found in paper form. As to validate that reasoning, a thorough search of the woman's home office turned up nothing but a few unpaid bills. None of them were overdue.

"Anything?" Sam asked from the doorway, frustrated.

"No. Maybe what we're looking for is at Day's place and he doesn't know it."

Her companion huffed in annoyance now as they drifted toward the kitchen.

"Let's talk this through," he said. "Treina finds evidence she thinks will keep her and her fiancé safe, then meets with Mossman's secretary to tell them to back off, trying to buy time until she and Day can take the evidence to the cops. Except Ott, or whoever, has already lined up a hit on her while Day is out of town. The robbery goes down and it looks like just another horrible street crime. 'Oh my, what a tragedy.'"

Susan was nodding her agreement even before he'd finished. "They didn't know Treina and Rob were engaged. They assumed he wasn't part of this. But why did they decide to kill him?"

Sam frowned. "Maybe the first time he tossed this place, Valens found something that told them she and Rob were getting married. That upped the stakes."

"Possible. They must have figured Treina'd have the evidence on her, and when she didn't, they turned Valens loose to find it. First he comes here. The cabbie's roommate was at home at the wrong time, the poor bastard. Then Valens rips up your hotel room. They already had issues with Day, worried he wasn't a 'team player', so they figure one little bomb and all their problems are solved. It'd be easy to blame his death on some disgruntled client, especially if that one had mob or cartel connections."

"You know, all that fits. But what lawyer would ever think they could get away with multiple murders?"

"A lawyer who's never been held accountable before," she replied.

They made their way back to the kitchen, where fingerprint

powder still coated various surfaces. At least the broken dishes had been swept up, though clearly Treina's family had bigger worries at this point.

Sam's phone pinged and he read the message, grinning as he typed a reply. "My contact at Treasury says that neither Mossman nor Warburg let the IRS know they had offshore bank accounts."

Susan smiled. "Well, at least that'll get them some serious federal heat."

"Not enough." He shook his head in defeat. " 'Heart' has to mean something if it's the first thing Treina said to her fiancée after nearly dying."

"I'm not seeing any hearts in this place," Susan replied, deflating. "Well, at least we got Valens. Maybe he'll squeal on whoever hired him, or the cops can trace his calls, unless he used a burner phone."

"Or it all might come down to Treina telling us where to find this heart of hers, once she's fully awake."

Beyond frustrated, Sam yanked on the pull cord to turn off the ceiling fan over the kitchen table. As he followed Susan to the front door, he frowned. Then stopped and turned.

The pendant at the end of the cord twirled in the air, catching the light from the window. Four steps got him back to the table, where he grabbed it, trapping it in his hand. He gave it a sharp tug and the heart broke into two pieces.

He held it up. "Hey! I found a heart. It's a data drive."

Susan whirled. "You're kidding me. We've been staring at that damned thing all along?"

"Maybe. Best to check it out on my computer before we celebrate," he said, carefully removing the other half of the heart from the pull cord. Mating the two parts, he tucked it into his jeans pocket. He made sure she didn't see him cross his fingers as she locked the door behind them.

Their chance to view the contents of the data drive without an audience vanished when they met Pat on the sidewalk. The detective wore a broad smile, one that promised good news.

"You know, I think you guys are going to win the lottery for the most 911 calls in a week," he said, joking. "Nice work catching Valens."

"Just doing our civic duty," Susan replied, then looked over at Sam.

He pulled out the heart and held it up.

"Jesus, is that it?" Pat asked.

"Don't know yet. Just about to give it a look over. Feel free to join us."

Susan and her ex bantered back and forth as Sam waited for his computer to boot up on the hood of Susan's car. Sadly, there was no shade, and the heat coming off the metal was hotter than he'd expected. Sweat formed on his forehead, not just a product of the temperature, and he wiped it away.

Once he'd logged in, he plugged in the thumb drive and clicked 'yes' to run a virus check. It went quickly and indicated the drive was clean.

"Showtime," he said, clicking on the drive icon. The others crowded up behind him, which reduced what little breeze there was. Sam sighed. "It needs a password," he said.

"Hold on." Susan dialed her partner, asked the question, then tapped her foot while she waited.

"She always like this?" Sam asked.

"Yup," Pat replied. "I've seen people on speed who are less energetic. For godsakes never let her drink espresso. Made that mistake once. Way too scary."

She gave both of them a hard stare, turned her back and walked a short distance away.

"Thanks for calling me about the explosion," Pat said quietly. "Appreciate that."

"I figured you'd want to know she was okay."

Susan kept tapping her foot until she got her answer, and then rejoined them. "Day says to try 'Rockstar0420.' It's the one she uses for her online bank account."

To Sam's relief, the password was accepted. "I'm in." Behind him, Susan began to hum the theme from *Jaws*. God, he adored this woman.

Only one file folder sat on the drive and it was labeled 'Neager.' Clicking on that revealed three individual file folders, which were labeled according to content: 'Financial,' 'Criminal,' 'Correspondence.' Inside those were individual files.

Realizing this was what they'd been looking for, Sam accessed his phone and turned on his personal hotspot. After doing a full backup of the drive into a special file folder on his computer, that info would now auto-sync with Veritas's server via his phone. "Susan, I'm sending a copy of this to your office e-mail in case it self-destructs the moment I open it. You want one too, Pat? I figure the more backups the better."

The detective nodded, then dropped a business card next to the computer with the required address. Sam typed it in and hit send. "Okay, now, let's see what we've got."

Sam clicked on the 'Financial' folder and found files, all of which documented individual wire transfers. He clicked on the first one, scanned through the information, and blinked. "Son of a bitch."

"Must be good—he doesn't swear that often," Susan said.

"He's going to be swearing more if he doesn't share what he found," Pat warned.

"This first one is the two-million-dollar transfer Day was talking about. It's to a numbered account in the Caymans." He clicked on the remaining five. "Same with the rest of these, each in differing amounts. It seems we have two distinct accounts here. I'm guessing one is Mossman's and the other, Warburg's."

He clicked on another folder, scanned the contents. "These are audio files. Each one also has a transcript. Probably the conversations in their private lounge, since it's bugged."

"Gotta love paralegals. They're great with the detail stuff," Susan said.

"We need to sit down and go through all this," Pat said.

"Agreed. Especially since the first few lines of this particular document mentions witness tampering, the fact that they have a mole in the state attorney general's office, and that they'll ensure that certain pieces of evidence go missing before the trial. Mossman says they have 'resources' in place to handle all of this," Sam reported.

"We have to be very careful about how we verify this information," the detective warned.

"Yeah, that's the tricky part. Mossman and Warburg are too savvy. One slip and they're free."

"Not if we go in with a warrant and find the original documents," Susan replied. "That, combined with Treina's testimony, might be enough."

"Think we can do that before all the evidence goes poof?" Sam asked.

"Only if we get damned lucky."

Chapter Thirteen

Friday, May 15th
Atlanta FBI Field Office
3:55 a.m.

Sam had worked some major cases in his time, but the pressure on this one was off the charts. Not knowing where the firm had all its moles, they'd set up shop at the Bureau's office, and only those who were working the case were allowed into the conference room.

The documents from Treina's thumb drive were printed out and shared between the homicide detectives, the agents, a trusted representative from the attorney general's office, and Susan's boss. One whiteboard was set up to document what evidence they had, another to track what they were missing and where they might find it. Then they went to work, assembling the puzzle, piece by piece.

He had fully expected to be told to run along like a good little boy, but that hadn't been the case. Rhodes had insisted he be here, and he'd accepted the invitation gracefully, knowing that it never would have been extended a couple weeks earlier.

"I think she likes me," he said under his breath to Britelli.

"Save an FBI agent's life and you're golden. It also didn't hurt that your boss called her right after the car bombing, offering his full support."

Crispin called Susan's boss? "How'd that go?"

"Rhodes didn't lose it, which surprised me. In fact, she thanked Wilder and then asked if he had any connections in the

Caymans, particularly in the banking industry."

"Crispin Wilder has connections *everywhere*."

"I believe that's what he told her. Hopefully those connections pay off."

"They will. They almost always do."

Sam was given the task of researching Valens's previous crimes, trying to find the link to the lawyers. He finally did after four hours' worth of digging through online records and court transcripts, and downing endless cups of coffee. It was a moment of personal pride for him when he presented his findings to Rhodes, knowing Susan was watching their interaction closely.

"Valens served time in California and moved to Georgia a couple months ago. His cellmate had been Mossman's confidential informant at one time. I'm willing to bet Valens's cellie told him get in touch with Mossman once he was here in Atlanta, just in case the sleaze needed something 'handled.'"

"Good bet. That gets us a connection, and we can work it from there." She paused. "Thank you."

Pleased, he returned to his chair. When he looked up, he saw Susan smiling. She gave him a discrete thumbs-up.

It was close to five in the morning when SAC Rhodes's phone rang. When she answered, she studied Sam, then pulled a notepad closer and began jotting down notes. After a brief conversation, he heard, "This was obtained legally? Okay. Then I appreciate your help."

When she rose, she looked as wrung out as the rest of them, caffeine no longer having the power to keep them going. They'd moved on to pizza, donuts, and now, sheer fortitude. With each passing hour, Sam felt they were running out of time. Sooner or later, someone would tell the lawyers that Valens was in custody. Probably already had.

Moving with renewed energy, Susan's boss walked to the whiteboard they'd been using to track the case's myriad of details. "I have had an individual with solid contacts in the Caymans verify that these accounts are indeed owned by

Mossman and Warburg." Selecting a red marker, she checked off each one of the wire transfers on that board. "We're looking at almost thirty million dollars, none of which was reported to the IRS." She looked back at them. "The folks at Treasury are rubbing their hands together in glee over that discovery. The penalties and interest will total into the millions."

Rhodes set the marker down. "The money transfers came from Neager's account, also offshore. Much smaller transfers were initiated from these two accounts and went to fourteen people here in the U.S. I have the list of those account holders." She looked over at the attorney general's representative. "One of them is from your office."

The guy groaned.

"There's also a sergeant in the APD, who I'm assuming has been supplying information to WMD on any cases involving them or their clients. I think we have enough to request the warrants for the law firm's office, as well as Mossman, Warburg, and Ott's homes."

The lawyer representing the attorney general rose as well. "Let me see what you've got, and then I'll call my boss."

"We'll need an impartial judge," Rhodes warned. "One who won't drop a dime on WMD."

"I know just the woman."

Sam looked over at Susan. She winked at him, then slumped forward, resting her head in her hands, exhausted. Yawning, he did the same, because nothing was more important than watching those warrants being executed. Not even sleep.

Warburg, Mossman and Day, P.C.
9:00 AM

As she pulled the car into the parking lot outside the law offices, Susan heard her companion yawn, loudly. "Some vacation you've had."

"That's for sure, though some parts have been stellar. In

particular, the time in your bed."

"Are you saying we need to do more of that sort of *sightseeing* before you leave?" she said.

"God, yes. Please."

"You know that might not happen, depending on how this case plays out."

"I know. We'll go with what we're given, but that won't keep me from bitching if there's no more 'us' time."

"Trust me, you won't be the only one."

Susan parked the car next to her boss's. Rhodes and Britelli were already out of their vehicles, as five other cars full of agents and support staff filled in around them, Pat and his partner as well. Randy looked pale after his bout of food poisoning.

Susan glanced up at the building. "They have to know we're coming. Can't hide a crew like this."

Stepping outside the vehicle, Sam re-tucked in his shirt, straightened his tie, then ran a hand through his hair.

"You ready for this?" she asked, shutting her door.

"Hell, yes."

Pat waved them over. "Got some good news and some not-so-good news. We've finally got a plea bargain in place with Valens now. Seems the threat of the death penalty loosened his mouth, and he gave us everything. His point of contact was Gail Ott. She arranged for the payments, all of it, but Mossman had a hand in the plans as well. Valens set up the deal with the cabbie so Treina Wilson was in the right place at the right time. And he copped to killing Myers's roommate because he was under orders to find the evidence, one way or another."

"Why would he think the roommate had it?"

Pat shrugged. "The guy isn't a Mensa candidate. He kept bitching about how he should have taken the drugs he'd found in the apartment, but Ott ordered him not to."

"Probably because she figured a chemically enhanced nutbar wasn't going to improve their situation," Susan replied.

Pat nodded. "And the not-so-good news?" she asked.

"He was shivved by another prisoner right before his

arraignment this morning. He's in the ICU and they're not sure if he'll make it or not."

Susan swore under her breath. "Tidying up those loose ends. It's what I'd do."

"At least we have Valens's confession," Pat replied. Which, they all knew, wasn't nearly as compelling as having the real deal on the witness stand.

The guard in the front lobby, confused by the mass of people in front of him, fell back on the rules and insisted someone sign in. Sam did the honors, along with delivering a warning against calling upstairs to let anyone know they had visitors.

When he got in the elevator with the others, Pat asked, "How did you sign the register?"

"The Heat," he replied. Exhausted laughter filled the car.

The immaculately clad receptionist never got out her "Good morning" before Rhodes and the detectives walked right past her. "Excuse me. Do you have an appointment?" she called out.

"We don't need one. We're the Heat," Pat said, grinning over at Sam.

Sam wasn't so sanguine. If either of the lawyers had been tipped off—and it was a good bet they had been, what with Valens's attack—every shred of evidence would be gone. The cops and the feds could still take them to court with what Treina had accumulated, but there were too many ways that could go wrong. Especially when your suspects were high-profile attorneys who were skilled at making witnesses vanish.

At the speed at which the courts moved, Treina and her fiancé would see their baby born before they had a chance to testify. The little guy might even be walking by the time his parents were called to the stand. And all that waiting time would be spent in a secure location, away from friends and family.

The double doors to the main office opened in front of them. Susan's boss took the lead, walking into the center of the room and holding up her badge. "I am Special Agent Rhodes of the Atlanta FBI office. We have a warrant to search the premises. You will all move away from your desks now. Leave your personal belongings right where they are."

"What did she say?" someone said.

"You're FBI?" another asked.

"Get the people out of their offices as quickly as you can," Rhodes ordered. "Begin with Warburg, Mossman, and Ott."

Sam found a wall upon which to lean as it all unfolded. It reminded him of one of those crime shows, except this was for real. People's lives were on the line here, as well as their careers—Susan's being one. There was no doubt a shitstorm of cosmic proportions would ensue if they didn't make this case stick.

Mossman and Warburg were found in their private meeting room and escorted out to the main part of the office, joined by Ott, as employees looked on in rapt astonishment. Warburg smiled genially, playing the quintessential gentleman, as if he'd been expecting their presence. If Day hadn't told them what the man was really like, Sam would have had a hard time believing he was a criminal. He was that smooth.

"Ma'am, how can I help you?" he asked, smiling as he headed toward Ms. Rhodes.

As soon as the lawyer drew closer, she slapped the legal documents into his hand. "We have a warrant to search these premises. You can help us by staying out of the way." Warburg's mouth opened, then closed. Apparently, he wasn't used to being told what to do in his own office.

To his dismay, none of them looked particularly worried.

They knew we were coming.

Sam shot a look at Susan, and from her frown, she was thinking the same thing. Which meant any evidence was probably long gone.

"Mr. Warburg?" Ms. Ott said, loudly enough for all to hear. "Do you want me to get the governor on the phone?"

"Not yet. I'm sure we can work this out," the older man said, playing to the crowd.

Rhodes didn't miss a beat. "The warrant allows us to secure

your computers, backups, files, both electronic and paper, and anything else in this office, right down to the paperclips."

"These are *confidential* client files," Warburg protested.

"Some are, some aren't. We have secured the services of an impartial attorney and he's onsite. He'll show us what we can and cannot take off the premises."

Glancing around, Sam found that most of the firm's employees seemed shell-shocked, but one wore a knowing smirk. It was the young man he'd seen on his first visit. He made his way over to Susan and whispered that information in her ear.

Her eyes went to the man he'd mentioned. "Thanks, I'll check him out."

Sam returned to the far wall as the agents did their work, rubbing a hand over his face. At least he and Susan had had a chance to shower and change clothes before pulling the all-nighter. She looked on fire now, and he knew this was what she lived for. He was the same.

This portion of the investigation was time consuming: logging in evidence, ensuring every little bit of paperwork was perfect so that evidence wasn't tossed when it reached the courtroom.

As he watched the process, he typed out a somber text to Veritas.

WARRANT EXECUTED. THEY WEREN'T SURPRISED WE'RE HERE.

The tension ran high, and Susan was feeling every bit of it. Her boss knew how to read people, and so Rhodes had already figured out that any incriminating evidence was history. Still, sometimes guilty people got sloppy when they were panicking. Or they kept their own copy of the evidence as a bargaining chip if they found themselves taking a fall for their bosses. Warburg and Mossman might not have felt the need to do that, but she bet Gail Ott did. Since she'd allegedly hired Valens, she'd need that evidence soon enough.

Acting on Sam's tip, Susan requested that one particular

employee be questioned up front—the young man who'd seemed pleased that his superiors were ass deep in federal agents. The man's name was Kevin Carmichael and he was head of the IT department. He didn't look like one's stereotypical geek, not with the black suit and pale-gray tie. Nevertheless, his expression spoke of a disdain for authority, or at least authority that made life miserable for him.

The young man took his place at the conference table, totally at ease. No guilt playing across his face at all. If anything, he appeared smug.

Susan sat across from Carmichael, Joe at her right side. Sam sat at her left, but had already indicated that he didn't intend to ask any questions unless absolutely necessary. She suspected he was worried that his involvement at this point might somehow taint the case when it went to court. If it did.

After explaining the recording procedure and gaining Carmichael's approval, Susan began.

"This interview is being conducted on May 15th, 2015 at nine forty-three in the morning, at the offices of Warburg, Mossman and Day, P.C., in Atlanta, Georgia. Present are Special Agents Britelli and Driscoll and Private Investigator Samuel Marsh. The interviewee is Mr. Kevin Carmichael." She took a hasty sip from a glass of water. "What do you do for the law firm, Mr. Carmichael?"

"The name's Kevin and I'm their IT wizard."

"Okay, Kevin. We couldn't help but notice you were smiling when Mr. Mossman was handcuffed. Any particular reason for that?"

"Other than he's an arrogant asshole?" the young man said.

"That might be considered a reason. Do you have any others?"

"Yes, I do. I'm in charge of internet security here. At five this morning, my phone alarm dinged. I have it set in case there's any attempt to hack the firm's files, or if any odd activity occurs after hours. Which in this case, it did."

"Is it company policy to monitor the system that closely?"

"No, it's the Carmichael policy. I'm the one who'll get

hosed if someone screws with something in-house, so I put protocols in place."

"Has this happened before?"

"Only once—some client's ex-husband tried to hack his way in. Busted him right off."

"Okay, so what was going on at five this morning?"

"Files were being purged on Ms. Ott's computer. Hers is password locked, so it had to be her or someone she trusts."

"How many people fall in that category?"

"Other than Mossman, nobody. But it was her, for sure."

"How do you know that?"

"The computer camera. I activated it when the alert came in."

Susan gave her partner a raised eyebrow. "Could you tell what was being purged?"

"Sure. It was a series of encrypted files. They were in a separate folder, away from the usual client files."

Oh, hell.

Kevin continued. "I was specifically told not to back up any encrypted files, no matter whose computer they were on. That they were of a personal nature, not related to the firm's business."

"So those files are gone?"

"No."

"No?" Susan asked. "You still have copies of them?"

"Sure do." He leaned his elbows on the desk. "Because if any of that stuff goes missing, I'd be blamed. The bosses would conveniently forget that they told me to ignore those files in the backup, and then I'd get fired and be denied unemployment benefits. Happened to a friend of mine at another firm, so I do backups of everything, no matter what."

Susan resisted the desire to execute a fist pump at that news.

"What level of encryption are we dealing with here?" Joe asked.

"Pretty basic. If it wasn't Ott, I'd say it was porn."

Susan decided not to comment on that, especially since this

was being taped. "Why do you dislike your bosses so much?"

"Warburg is a horny old goat, likes to grope the secretaries. Mossman's a jerkoff," Kevin said matter-of-factly. "Said he didn't know why they paid me so much when a trained monkey could do my job."

Susan whistled. Never piss off the computer geeks. They had so many ways to make your life a living hell.

"Can you supply us with copies of those encrypted files?" she asked.

"Sure. But there's no need. You're taking Ott's computer as evidence, right?"

"Yes."

"Well, the files are on there."

"But you said they were deleted," she replied, confused.

"The protocol does a full backup at four every morning in case any of our attorneys pulled late-night hours. Right after that, it verifies that what's on the firm's computers matches what's in the backup, because sometimes the legal guys aren't computer savvy and mess something up. The protocol ensures data isn't lost."

"Which means?"

"Any missing files are automatically restored to the individual's computer, in a separate folder. That way those can be reviewed, and either saved in the proper place or junked."

It took a minute for Susan to realize what he'd said.

"You're sure all those files are back on Ott's computer?" Joe asked, astounded.

"Sure am. I checked right before you guys hit the door, wondering what she was up to. I just couldn't believe it when y'all walked in. Made my freaking year."

It all made sense now. "You were helping Treina Wilson, weren't you?"

Kevin looked down at the table, then back up at them. "Yeah. I hacked Ott's password and gave it to Treina. When she told me what she thought was going on, I knew I had to help her."

"Why didn't you call us when she got shot?"

Now he looked chagrined. "I thought it was just a robbery gone bad. Then, the more I thought about, I began to wonder."

"Thank you, Kevin. We appreciate your help," Susan said.

"As long as those bastards go to jail, I'm happy."

She ended the recording, then said, "You know you're most likely going to be out of a job when this is over."

He shrugged. "I started my own gaming company two years back. It's big enough now I don't need this job. I just stayed to help Treina. When I heard Mossman bitching about the FBI asking questions, I knew it was only a matter of time before you guys showed up."

It took only a short time for one of the FBI's data analysts to access Ott's computer files. Kevin had supplied the password, but swore he'd not read the contents as Treina had warned him it might been dangerous for him to know what was really going on. He'd believed her.

Once Susan had verified the files' contents matched those on Treina's thumb drive, she knew they were on solid ground. Keeping her grin hidden, she found Rhodes talking to one of the agents and pulled her aside. After she delivered the good news, her boss stared at her for a few seconds as if she couldn't believe what she'd just heard.

"We have everything?" Susan nodded. "*Damn*, Christmas did come early this year. Remind me to be nicer to the geeks at the office."

"So how are you going to handle this?"

"Ott is the weak link. The suits have no respect for her, that's obvious. She needs to see that they'll happily let her face the death penalty to save their own necks." She paused. "Let me tell the cops what's up first."

While Rhodes pulled the two detectives aside for a private conversation, Susan joined Sam.

"How'd it go?" he asked, his voice barely above a whisper.

"Damn good," she said, keeping her expression neutral. "Thanks for the tip about the IT guy. We have what we need."

"Will that earn me special privileges when we get back to

your place?" he asked, his voice huskier now.

She felt heat flare inside her. "Sure will. There are still a lot more sights for you to see."

He blew out a stream of air. "Man, I love this town."

She laughed and then returned to stand near her boss. Now came the part she loved.

As all this action had swirled around them, the three main suspects had been parked in leather chairs just outside Warburg's office. Mossman's eyes tracked Susan's every movement, while Ott just stared at nothing.

Right on cue, Pat stepped up, cuffs in hand. "Gail Ott?" Her head swung up, eyes wide. "I'm placing you under arrest for murder."

"What? No!" she began. "Ed, what are they doing?"

"Just keep cool, Gail. We'll get this sorted out," Mossman replied.

"You said—"

"Just keep your cool," he repeated. "It'll be fine."

Joe stepped up to him now. "Edward Mossman, you're under arrest."

"On what charges?"

"We'll start with jury tampering and witness intimidation, and take it from there. That work for you?"

Susan bit her tongue, trying not to laugh, as it was her turn. With a quick glance at Sam, she walked over to the oldest lawyer. "Mr. Warburg, you are under arrest. You have the right to remain—"

"Don't bother," the man spat as he surged out of his chair. "I was defending clients before you were born."

Susan kept talking, finishing the warning. Even as he agreed that he understood his rights, Warburg kept staring at her. "What is your name?"

"Special Agent Susan Driscoll."

There were a gasps from a few of the employees who'd probably read about her in the local newspaper after the Ellers incident. Not surprising since her name had been in the news for over a week.

"I'm going to remember you, do you understand me?" Warburg said, his eyes steely. The threat was wrapped in a velvet glove, but it was still there.

"Good to hear your memory's in fine shape, sir. Guys your age often have trouble with that. And *other* things."

There were snickers from a couple of the secretaries now as Warburg's face flushed crimson.

"Charlie," Mossman warned. "She's baiting you."

The old man continued to glower. "So it appears."

Ms. Ott twitched, noticeably. Warburg noticed. "We have nothing to worry about. I'll talk to the governor and he'll see that we're not harassed any further."

"Don't bother. I already talked him," Rhodes said. "He said he'll be sure to allow the judicial system to move forward unimpeded." She looked over at Ott now. "Though it does seem that your partners intend on throwing you under the bus."

"No, they wouldn't do that," Ott replied, but her voice sounded unsure.

"That's not what they said when they were in that private lounge of yours this morning. Do I need to share that conversation with you? Because it's all on tape."

Though Susan suspected it was a total bluff, Ott's face turned alabaster, swinging toward her two bosses now. "You bastards. You lying bastards! You said everything would be okay."

"Gail, you need to calm down," Mossman said.

"The hell I'm going to calm down. You're not going to throw me to the wolves. That's not happening."

Warburg sneered. "I knew you were incompetent. The only reason you have a job is that you're good on your knees."

Susan whistled. *Ouch.*

Ott's expression grew cold. "You'll pay for that one, old man. Oh, will you pay."

"Both of you shut up!" Mossman demanded.

Ott ignored him and took a step toward Rhodes. "I want a deal," she said. "I know exactly what these two have done, and I'll tell you all of it, but I want a deal."

"You bitch!" Mossman bellowed, immediately forgetting his own advice. When he lurched toward her, Joe manhandled him back into his chair, as the man issued a string of curses.

God, I love this.

As Ott was escorted from the room, she slowed as she walked by Sam. "You just *had* to play good Samaritan, didn't you?"

He nodded. "Damned glad I did."

Mossman and Warburg were led out shortly thereafter, in the custody of a few of the junior agents. Both were scowling and Susan suspected whatever paper thin loyalty they had to each other wasn't going to survive time in a jail cell.

It was only after they were out the door that one of the secretaries cried, "Yes! Now that was a perp walk!" A couple others began clapping, though most still appeared shellshocked.

Rhodes waved Susan over, pensive now.

"That worked better than I thought it would."

"Damned awesome to watch," Susan replied.

"Look, you and the PI did the heavy lifting at the start of the investigation; the rest of us will take it from here. Be back in the office Monday morning. If I see you before then, well, just don't do it. You understand, Special Agent Driscoll?"

Susan blinked. "Ah, yes, ma'am. Monday morning it is."

"Good. Now get the hell out of here."

Sam was already heading for the door, wearing the widest grin imaginable.

Chapter Fourteen

Susan's Apartment
6:15 p.m.

Once they'd reached her apartment, they'd made love in the shower, then in the kitchen while she baked them chocolate chip cookies to eat with their ice cream. Finally, they reached the bed, and after another round of breathless climaxes, exhaustion claimed both of them.

Now Sam lay on his left side, his back to her, the sheet down below his hip, murmuring in his sleep. She kissed his shoulder, trailing her hand down his arm. Slowly he woke, then rolled toward, his hair tousled and his eyes bright.

"God, you're beautiful," Sam said, pulling her toward him. "And right now you're mine. All mine. I'm such a selfish bastard, I refuse to share."

She knew that when Samuel Marsh finally left her behind, her heart would bleed for the loss of his mischievous smile, his soothing touch, and his very generous loving.

Hartsfield-Jackson
Atlanta International Airport
Sunday, May 17th
4:10 p.m.

In the end, Susan had insisted that they return his rental car and she'd take him to the airport. Sam had agreed, wanting to spend as much time with her as possible. Nevertheless, the drive to the airport was too quiet. They both knew that one wrong word might collapse everything they'd built over the last few days. One right word, and the foundation would grow stronger. With each lovemaking, each laugh, each shared memory, the bond between them had grown. Would it hold when he was hundreds of miles away, or would the connection fray and disintegrate?

He'd never felt such pressure when it came to a woman. Susan Driscoll was what he'd been looking for, and now he was going to leave her behind. It was the first time he'd regretted accepting Veritas's offer.

Susan pulled up to the curb at Hartsfield-Jackson's South Terminal. Putting the car in park, she stared ahead, not at him.

"This isn't easy," she said, voicing exactly what he was thinking.

"No, it's not," he said, unlatching his seatbelt. "It doesn't have to end here, honey. There's too much between us, and I don't mean the investigation."

Those gorgeous brown eyes moved to him now, and he experienced a faint stir of hope. "You felt it too?" Sam nodded. "So it wasn't me just building fairy tale castles in the air?"

"No, it wasn't."

She looked out her window, watching as a taxi went by. "I'm going to be job hunting once we get the WMD case filed."

"But I thought you never wanted to move away from here. Georgia peach, remember?"

"I don't want to move, but . . . I do," she replied, looking back at him now. "Rhodes is being more human, but I can't be sure that's going to continue. I love this city, but I want to spread my wings. See what the world has to offer. I need a change."

"You staying with the FBI?"

She nodded. "I know, there's a Bureau office in Chicago."

"Well, wherever you go, make sure you're happy, and that it has an airport so I can visit you. Or you can visit me."

"What? No sales pitch for the Windy City?"

Before he could reply, there was a tap on his side window. An Atlanta cop motioned them to move on.

Susan rolled down the window. "FBI—official business," she said.

"Got some way to prove that?" the man asked politely.

"I do." She retrieved her badge and held it up.

The cop gave it a quick glance, then nodded. "Have a fine day, ma'am," he said and walked off as the window went back up.

Silence engulfed them now, as if they'd lost something with the interruption. Finally, Sam touched her arm.

"Go where you have to go, do what you have to do. Just remember that I'll be there for you."

From the deep emotion in her eyes, that had been what she wanted to hear.

Susan put her fingers over the top of his. "Thank you. That means so much to me. I've . . . never felt this close to someone I just met. I don't really want to lose that, Sam, but I'm afraid I might. Which makes me wonder if my career is worth it."

He gave her a reassuring smile. "My mom always claims that love works out the way it should. So I'm going to trust her on this one. Somehow, we'll find a way to be together."

She seemed bewildered now. "You talked to your parents about me?"

"Not yet, but I want to. I want you to meet them. That's how serious I am about us."

"Okay, but sometime down the line," she said. "Call me when you get to Chicago. Call me anytime. I might not be able to answer, but I'll know you're thinking of me."

"Same here, honey. Let's make this a beginning, not an end."

After long kiss, which only made it harder for him to let her go, Sam finally exited the car, shutting the door behind him. He paused for a moment, debating whether anything was worth leaving Susan behind.

Finally, he blew her another kiss, seeing the tears rolling down her cheeks. With a heavy sigh, and a heavier heart, Sam walked into the terminal, rolling his suitcase, alone.

Veritas's Headquarters
Chicago, Illinois
Friday, July 3rd
2:45 p.m.

The nearly seven weeks since Sam had left Atlanta had been consumed by one project: the background research for a potential mission, one that Crispin had ordered him to keep secret, at least for the time being.

Sam had readily complied and thrown himself into the work, if for nothing more than to try to disguise his loneliness. Every second without Susan was penance, like a prison sentence with no end in sight. They'd remained in touch by phone, e-mail, and texts. He'd even sent her goofy greeting cards and flowers, but it wasn't enough.

Now, as he waited for Crispin's input on his report, he scrutinized the weapon hanging on the wall behind his boss. It'd intrigued him from the first time he'd seen it. Sam expected a man who'd once been an international arms dealer to be up to his eyes in firearms, and no doubt, there were a few hidden in this room. Still, to have a broadsword in plain sight made a statement, especially since Sam had heard this melee weapon wasn't just for decoration.

Wilder's brown hair was pulled back in its usual ponytail, and today he was wearing a white shirt and black slacks. The shirtsleeves were rolled up, and his tan was fading. Too many hours in the office. Too much weight on his shoulders. Sam had been pleased to hear that Morgan was going to take on some of that load now. Crispin needed the help.

His boss looked up. "Impressive. You went really deep on this one."

Sam kept his sigh of relief silent. "I got the sense that the stakes were higher than usual, and that's saying a lot."

Crispin nodded, tapping a finger on the file. "If we green-light this mission, it can't have any surprises since the lead operative is not one of our regular team."

Sam nodded, understanding. "If we do take it on, it's a worthy one. The fact that parents are still entrusting their kids to so-called military boot camps, then having some of those same teens come home in a coffin is criminal. I found too many cases where no one ever saw a day in jail for those deaths. Somehow, people just shrugged and moved on, like the kids were expendable just because they might be troublemakers."

"I agree. Once a decision is made, file all your expenses for reimbursement. But right now, let's keep this quiet for a bit longer. Certain people in our organization are *not* going to be happy about this mission once they realize who would be leading it."

That was an understatement.

Crispin leaned back in his chair, interlacing his hands behind his head. "How goes it with our favorite FBI agent in Atlanta? Has Ms. Driscoll found a new position yet?"

The topic shift caught Sam off guard. "Susan's still interviewing. She says she's got a couple strong possibilities and has been called back for second interviews. She's looking for just the right boss and office environment."

"I'm sure she'll find one. Ms. Driscoll is very good at what she does."

Sam smiled. "Yes, she is. The last I heard was that Ms. Ott plea-bargained with the best of them. Her documents backed up the ones Ms. Wilson had obtained, along with a few new ones that moved the charges solidly into RICO territory. The feds popped a bottle of champagne over that."

"That's great news. If Ms. Driscoll decides not to stick with the Bureau, let me know. She'd be an perfect addition to our staff, especially now that Morgan is taking on more administrative duties."

"Has Alex popped the question yet?" Sam asked.

"Not that I've heard of. If he keeps delaying, she will probably ask him. Her patience is wearing thin."

He laughed. "I can see that happening."

Crispin tapped the report on his desk again. "I'll be sure to go through this dossier again over the weekend and let you know if I have any follow-up questions. Oh, and if I've not said it yet, thank you for joining us full-time. You're a highly skilled investigator, and I'm very grateful to have you on our team."

The praise felt good. "Thank you. That's means a lot to me. I am so impressed with the work we do here."

"As am I."

Sam rose. "Well, enjoy your Fourth of July holiday, sir."

"I shall try. Do you have any plans?" Crispin asked.

"Not really." *Not when I'm missing the one person who would make it special.*

"Well, perhaps your weekend will be better than you anticipate," his boss said.

Puzzled at that last statement, Sam shut the door and headed back to his own office to face a long weekend alone. In years past, that wouldn't have mattered. Now that he'd met Susan, it meant everything.

North Michigan Avenue
Chicago
5:30 p.m.

As the cab crossed the river, Susan dialed a number she knew by heart. Sam immediately answered.

"Hey, lady. So where are you today?" he asked. He sounded uncommonly tired. That weariness had been growing over the last few weeks, as if he'd given up hope she'd ever visit him.

"I'm in Chicago."

There was utter silence for a few seconds. "Chicago?" he blurted.

"Yup. I was in the neighborhood and figured I'd visit my boyfriend. You think he'd be up for that?"

The shout on the other end of the phone nearly deafened

her.

When Sam regained control, he said, "I think he would. Are you at the airport? If you give me a while, I can meet you there and get you back to my place."

"No need. I just crossed the river, headed your direction. Should be at your condo in a few minutes."

"What?" More silence. "Ah, I'm not home right now. I'm in the Osaka Garden. That's way south of you. Ah, it'll take thirty minutes, at least, depending on how fast I can catch a cab."

His panic was so sweet. "No problem. I'll just wait in the lobby."

She heard the sound of hurried footsteps on pavement, like he was running.

"Oh, God, I can't believe it!" Sam said, his breath shorter as the sound of footsteps picked up speed. "You're here. In Chicago. To see me."

"I am." That wasn't the only reason she was in this town, but she'd save that bit of news for later. "Figured you would know how to show me a good time over the holiday weekend."

"Oh, honey, you have . . . no idea," he said, his voice deeper now. The sound of it sent welcome shivers across her skin. "I'll be there ASAP. I'll let . . . the doorman know . . . you're coming."

Then he was gone. Susan put the phone back in her purse, smiling. Any worries she'd had about whether Sam had missed her had just been shot down in flames.

The one day he'd decided not to stick around home after work. No, he'd been so morose he'd headed down to Jackson Park for some time in the beautiful Japanese gardens. The place always restored his soul. Silly him, if he'd stayed home, his soul would have been happier a lot sooner.

She's in Chicago!

Sam frantically waved down a cab, then jumped in. In between gulps of air, he gave the cabbie his address.

"Sure. You okay, buddy?" the man asked, eyeing him in the

rearview mirror as he headed back into traffic.

"Girlfriend just got into town." Another gulp of air. "Didn't know she was coming. Been forever."

The cabbie smiled. "Good weekend planned, then."

"Yeah, hell yes, the best."

She came to Chicago to see me.

In that simple gesture, Sam knew what they had was real. Now he just had to ensure she knew it.

Sam's Condo
5:45 p.m.

Once out of the cab, Susan peered up at the building. It was older, but well maintained, probably built in the 1950s, and located a short distance from Lake Michigan. As she entered the lobby, the guard looked up, then gave her a big smile like he knew her.

"You have to be Ms. Driscoll."

"Ah, yes."

"Mr. Marsh called, said you were headed this way. Also said I was to give you the spare keys and the alarm code so you can go right up. This time of night, lord knows when he'll get up here from Jackson Park."

"Okay, that works."

"If you could just sign in here," he said, indicating a sheet.

She rolled over her suitcase and performed the deed.

"He said you were really pretty, and he got that right. Mr. Marsh usually doesn't say anything about his ladies, so that tells me he thinks you're special."

That pleased her immensely. "Good, I think the same of him." Susan accepted the keys and a piece of paper with the alarm code.

"You have a great weekend, ma'am."

"Same to you."

When she reached the ninth floor, it took no time to find

the condo—it was at the end of the hall, and from the layout, it appeared to be a corner apartment. Susan opened the door, found the alarm panel, and typed in the code. Then heaved a sigh of relief when the panel stopped beeping. After the door closed behind her, she wheeled her suitcase into the condo. And gasped.

"Wow! Look at this place!" she said.

Laying her purse on a nearby chair, she walked into the center of the large room. Besides the stunning open-plan architecture, there was a long bank of windows facing the lake. Those continued on around the corner to the south, as well, adding even more real estate to the million-dollar view.

Susan walked the entire length of those windows, which overlooked both Lakeshore Drive below and Lake Michigan just beyond. She could imagine what it would be like at sunrise or during a thunderstorm. Even during the winter. Sam had claimed he had a decent view, but hadn't said it was stunning.

"Oh you silly man, a decent view is not having to see the parking lot." This was heaven.

Turning, Susan found that the kitchen was open plan as well, which meant you could cook dinner and see the lake at the same time.

"Damn, Marsh. You've got excellent taste."

Wandering through the kitchen, she ran her hand over the black granite countertop. This place was ideal if you wanted to have friends over for drinks or a meal. Shaking herself out of her serious case of condo lust, she glanced at the clock on the far wall. If she was lucky, she'd have time to get cleaned up before Sam arrived.

Grabbing her suitcase and purse, Susan headed down the hallway. A bedroom on the right, half bath on the left. A smaller bedroom that was now an office. To her delight, the master bedroom had the same big windows and a deliciously large bathroom. The shower was large enough for four.

"Oh yeah, this is so gonna work," she said, turning in a circle. "Weekend, here we come!"

Sam tried not to wrench open his apartment door in his eager-
ness, but failed.

"Susan?"

There was no reply, but he heard the shower running, which
meant his timing had been perfect. Stripping off his clothes,
letting them fall every which way down the hall, he tapped on
the bathroom door, then entered. Through the water-streaked
shower door, Susan's lithe body appeared like an impressionist
painting. All curves and lines and rosy nipples.

"Susan?"

She turned. "There you are."

He opened the door, stepped inside, and was welcomed by
a stream of hot water and the arms of a very sexy and aroused
woman. *His* woman.

"I've *really* missed you, Sam. All of you," she said, taking
a nip at his earlobe as her hand went in search of one of the
parts of him that had been missing her. She smelled like his
soap and he was hard in an instant. Her fingers rubbing along
his shaft only made him harder. "Now show me how much
you've missed me. And for God's sake, don't go slow."

He knew that tone, knew what it meant, and loved it when
it happened. Then he swore; his supply of condoms was not in
the shower with them. As he turned to retrieve one, she waved
a packet in front of his nose.

"Thank God," he said.

The seduction went down exactly as she'd commanded.
After a sharp suckling of one of her breasts, which elicited
a deep moan, he ran his hand down her water-slicked skin
and into her curls. She was more than ready for him, pushing
against his fingers, her eyes closed.

"Missed me, huh?" he teased.

"Sam . . . " she warned.

He knew she'd tackle him if he didn't step up to the plate.
After sheathing himself, he braced her against the tile, then slid
into her, deep enough to make her gasp. She moaned, hot and
wet, her heat burning around him. The world narrowed down to
just them: the water hitting their skin, her cries as he took her,

the slide of flesh against flesh, the rising heat in his groin.

"Harder!" she cried, her head back, the water sheeting off her face, her lips swollen from his kisses.

Hitching her legs around his waist, he took her as she wanted: fast and without compromise. Claiming her as his own. Later, he'd make love to her again, slowly, thoroughly, exquisitely. Now, they were reigniting the passion between them in the most primitive of ways, and it felt incredible.

Susan's cries in the shower rose as her core muscles tightened around him, pulling him, urging him toward his own climax. Closing his eyes, Sam bellowed as he exploded inside her. Once it was over, still breathing heavily, Susan's legs slowly slid down his. He kept his hand on her waist to ensure she didn't lose her footing.

"That was . . . " she began.

"Incredible," he said, cupping her face and kissing her forehead. "*You* are incredible. God, how I've missed you."

When she looked up at him, he saw something he'd never seen before. Something he'd prayed for. Somehow, instinctively, he knew the time was right.

"I'm falling in love with you, Susan," he said, gazing into those whiskey-brown eyes that had captured his heart. "Please tell me you're feeling the same about me."

For a second, she didn't reply. Then Susan leaned her head against his chest and whispered, "Of course I am. You're the one I've been praying for."

Sam felt the hot sting of tears and was grateful the shower would hide them. After turning off the water, he bundled her into a towel and guided her to the bed. Once he'd dealt with the shield, they lay together, light fingers stroking each other's damp skin.

Sam's life had changed that morning when he'd opened his hotel room door. It could have been anyone on the other side, but instead it'd been Susan. His heart had found someone to love, an equal, a woman of such strength that he would always be in awe of her.

Epilogue

Millennium Park
8:00 p.m.

"The Bean, huh?" Susan asked, peering up at this curiously shaped sculpture made of polished stainless steel. It was cool how it reflected both the buildings in the distance, and the people nearby.

"Officially, it's Cloud Gate, but everyone just calls it The Bean because of its shape," Sam explained.

Once they'd risen from their bed, he'd brought her downtown to Millennium Park, to see this bean thing. The longer Susan studied it, she had to admit it was unique, and a lot less creepy than the tall, tower-like fountains that spouted water out of people's faces. Still, Chicago did have a vibe, and she found herself tapping into it. Part of it was Sam's near child-like enthusiasm to show her his city. The other was that she actually liked the place.

"So, what do you think of my town?" he asked.

"Pretty neat, even if I haven't yet seen one statue of a Confederate general."

He laughed, slipping his arm around her waist. "There's one in Oak Woods Cemetery on the South Side."

"Oh good. I was worried there for a moment," she said.

"I really do love the dress," he said, eyeing her closely now. "When did you buy it?"

"A couple days after you left. I wanted something to remind me of you."

"Glad you did. You look great in it." He tightened his grip on her waist. "How're Treina and her guy doing?"

"Well, she's about halfway through her pregnancy; they found a new apartment and have the nursery all set up. Luckily, with Ott turning state's evidence they didn't need witness protection. Oh, and I've been invited to a baby shower."

"Better you than me," he said, smiling. "I've heard horror stories about those things."

Susan's phone rang and she disentangled herself to retrieve it from her purse. Glancing at the number, her heart sped up. "Sorry, I gotta take this."

Sam sat on the nearest bench, watching her pace. That was so her style; Susan rarely stood still. All that energy in one beautiful bundle. He hadn't been blowing smoke about the dress—it looked great on her. The way the sun caught her hair, the swell of her breasts, her long legs. How they'd been wrapped around him as they'd found their release together in the shower, and in his bed.

Damn, I'm so lucky.

As she continued to talk, he tried to translate her expression, but when she caught him watching her, she turned her back on him. It was well past five on a holiday weekend, so it was unlikely to be one of the FBI offices calling her. Which left family or maybe Joe checking on her. Hopefully it had nothing to do with the WMD case.

Susan ended the call, put the phone in her purse, and then just stared into the distance. Worried, he joined her.

"Everything okay?"

She looked up at him, her eyes moist. "I just got a job offer."

"That's great news! But why are you upset?"

"I'm not. I'm just overwhelmed. It seems all my dreams are coming true recently."

"I know the feeling," he said, touching her cheek.

"The office that offered me the job is the one I'd hoped would come through. I really liked the SAC, liked the way the other agents interacted with him and each other. They felt like a team. So I accepted the job."

Sam swore his heart missed a few beats. This was good news, right? "Okay, lay it on me. Where are we moving?"

She blinked at him. "We?"

"We. I can't stand being away from you, honey. The last few weeks, I've been going crazy without you, so if you want, I'm willing to move to wherever you are."

"You'd actually leave Chicago?" she asked, incredulous.

"Yes," he said, not thrilled, but knowing this was what loving someone was all about. He'd miss Chicago—hell, he'd be lost outside of this town—but in time, he'd find another job. Or maybe Veritas could use him even if he lived in wherever the hell they were going.

His bottom line: Susan was all that mattered.

"You'd sell that gorgeous condo for me?"

He winced. "Yes. We'll find another one. Can't be the only one in the world."

"Those are *big* sacrifices, Sam. I know how much you love this city, and your work with Veritas."

"I'd give them up for you. That's what this is all about. I love you."

She looked down, taking his hands in hers. Tears were brimming in her eyes now, and he reached up and wiped them away as they ran down her cheeks.

"So where am I moving?" he pressed. "Seattle? Dallas? Please tell me it's not D.C. The traffic there is a bitch."

She laughed. "No moving needed, at least for you."

"What?" His heart began to pound. She didn't want him with her?

"The job I accepted is here, in Chicago."

"Here? *Chicago*?"

She nodded again, then cautiously wiped away her tears. "I didn't tell you I interviewed here because I didn't want you to get your hopes up. The second interview was this morning. Apparently, the SAC wanted to finalize the offer before the weekend. Said I was too valuable to lose to another office. He really wants me to be part of his team."

"Chicago," he murmured.

Then he had his arms around her, twirling her in a circle, laughing the entire time. When he set her on the ground, Sam framed her face with his hands and kissed her. Wolf whistles came their way from some of the others in the park.

"I'd love you even if we were moving to Portland or Des Moines or wherever."

"Yeah, but you love me more *here*. Admit it."

"Damned straight," he said. "So, how do we celebrate this great news? Fancy dinner out? French? Italian? German?"

"Pizza."

"Okay. But tomorrow night, I'll fix us supper at my place. Then we can curl up and watch the fireworks."

"You got it." She laid a kiss on his nose. "Okay, Chicago dude, show me this pizza you keep raving about. It better be damned special or there's going to be payback."

"This from a woman who thinks haute cuisine is boiled peanuts?"

"Hey, enough with the trash talking," she said, linking her arm through his. "That's my state nut you're dissing."

"State nut. Don't get me started."

She laughed and he joined in. Once they reached the street, he gave a sharp whistle and a wave. To her surprise, a taxi glided up to the curb in front of them. Sam opened the rear door, always the gentleman.

"Time to show you my town, sweetheart."

She knew she'd never be in safer or more loving hands.

Sam's Condo
Saturday, July 4th
9:30 p.m.

Curled up on the sofa, they rested while they waited for the fireworks to begin. The day had been full—Sam had taken her to the Chicago History Museum, insisting she had to know all about her new home, then down to the Art Institute. They'd had lunch along the river, and then he'd cooked supper, a truly gourmet meal of baked salmon, roasted potatoes, and freshly grilled mushrooms. In between all that, they'd made love in his big bed.

In the distance, a high burst of light broke the darkness as the fireworks began. Sam had left the windows open, so they could almost hear the music from Navy Pier. The roar of the crowd carried much farther. Another burst, this one in reds and blues and incandescent whites.

"This is why I bought the place. No need to fight the traffic," he said.

"It's gorgeous. Pity it only happens once a year."

He laughed. "You kidding? There're fireworks two or three times *a week* throughout the summer. Chicago never goes halfway on anything."

"What? Then why didn't you just kidnap me in May and drag me up here? I love fireworks."

"You needed to make this decision on your own."

He was right, of course.

"By the way, to suggest that the *only* reason you're going to be living with me is because of Chicago's frequent pyrotechnic displays, is a substantial blow to my male ego."

She smirked. "Well, there is the view and the kitchen. Oh, and the big shower is pretty compelling as well." Then she poked him in the chest. "Don't worry, there's nothing wrong with your male *anything*, Mr. Marsh. I would know. I've run a thorough test of all that equipment, and *your* pyrotechnics are in peak condition."

In the distance, the latest burst formed into a brilliant red and blue heart.

She quirked a dubious eyebrow. "Okay, that was corny."

"No, that's romantic, honey. I asked them to do that one specially."

"You're lying."

"Maybe. But it's still romantic."

Susan opened her mouth to protest, and he found the most perfect way to stop her. By the time they'd ceased making their own explosions, the other fireworks display was nearly over.

"Welcome to Chicago, my lily," he whispered, laying her head on his chest as they rested, all tangled together, body and soul.

Susan snuggled closer, sensing the endless love that surrounded her. "Welcome home, Sam."

THE END

Mission Notes

Before Veritas undertakes a mission, a comprehensive background dossier is created to get the "lay of the land." This was not the case in regard to the events in Atlanta involving Samuel Marsh and FBI Agent, Susan Driscoll.

Because the mission was not originally sanctioned, but undertaken as events played out, there was great concern as to precisely what this situation required. At stake was a potential clash with a major law firm and the Federal Bureau of Investigation.

Through Crispin Wilder's numerous contacts, as well as Samuel Marsh's, information was received regarding Warburg, Mossman and Day PC, the legal firm that employed the victim.

WMD, as they were called, had a history of helping their clients escape prosecution for such crimes as racketeering, money laundering and wire fraud. Those alone would warrant Veritas' scrutiny. The attempted murder of a witness to their crimes ensured it.

About the Author

Jana Oliver never planned to become an author. In fact, she told her sixth grade teacher she wanted to be an international spy, which sounded very cool at the time.

That so didn't happen.

After pursuing various careers (registered nurse, disc jockey, travel agent, copywriter) someone flipped a switch in her brain and stories began to pour out. There were so many stories she decided to write them down and publish them. Then someone else published them, in the U.S. and then all over the world.

She's still surprised by all that.

A few years down the line Jana's an international bestselling author with over twenty books to her credit, and has won over a dozen major writing awards, including the Maggie Award of Excellence, the Daphne du Maurier, National Readers Choice and the Prism Award.

Nowadays she can be found writing her tales in Portugal when not sharing time with her very patient husband and their cranky (ghost) Feline Overlord, Ms. Dali.

www.JanaOliver.com

Also by Jana Oliver

DEMON TRAPPERS® SERIES
Forsaken (formerly The Demon Trapper's Daughter)
Forbidden (formerly Soul Thief)
Forgiven
Foretold
Grave Matters
Mind Games
Valiant Light
Lost Souls
Bitter Magic

TIME ROVERS® SERIES
Sojourn
Virtual Evil
Madman's Dance

VERITAS SERIES
Cat's Paw
Killing Game
Broken Dreams

DRAGONFIRE SERIES
The Circle of the Swan
The Healer's Path
The Summoning Stone
The Lore of Dragons

STANDALONE NOVELS & NON-FICTION
Briar Rose
Dead Easy
Tangled Souls
Socially Engaged: The Author's Guide to Social Media
(co-authored with Tyra Burton)